ISBN: 978-1-7397172-0-9

Ghost Story

BARBARA COOPER

Ratmulen House

November 2nd , 1927

HE COULD HEAR THE LARGE CHURCH BELLS FROM TOWN RINGING BEHIND HIM. It was late, the sun had just set in a glorious bloody sunset, as if it didn't want to give up, fighting until its last breath while splashing the sky red and a golden hue of orange.

It was already evening, he felt sorry he hadn't gone sooner.

He was in a hurry to get to the graveyard. And in a hurry to leave this god-forsaken place behind him afterwards. But one thing he was taking with him this time - her - his lover.

Just one visit. Last visit to his parents' grave. He didn't like this time of year, he braced himself against the cold. The church which he had now arrived at, small and forgotten, was quiet. Fragrant with the smell of fall.

The night now quickly embraced everything into a thick veil of darkness. He walked into the graveyard. Everything here was alight, every grave was set with burning candles from parishioners. He walked between the tombstones, along small pathways, he knew the way, <u>he always knew the way.</u> To his mother's and father's grave.

To say goodbye. He set ablaze his own candle he brought with him, just for them. Today, while he can still be here.

1

His fine automobile is ready, standing in a getaway mode waiting.

One of the luxuries he now has – oh, how he would have wanted to share that with his parents.

He must head back to the house, the manor.

There, she is waiting for him.

They are leaving tonight.

He heard a loud crash suddenly. Not knowing where it came from, he turned his head to the not faraway trees, in the direction of the ocean.

Feeling suddenly as if his heart might be breaking into a million little pieces. Is that even possible?

Prologue

October 1996
Sebastian

THE DOOR BLEW OPEN AND A STRONG GUST OF WIND CAME INTO THE ROOM.

He didn't mind: he was having fun. The wooden floor creaked. Otherwise, the room was nice and cosy. The fire blazed in the corner.

Someone got up and closed the door.

The girls were giggling and covering their mouths and faces with their well-manicured hands.

The party – a small group of people gathered around the table – was underway and it was lively.

He wasn't feeling cold, on the contrary he was warm.

The women kept laughing, and encouraging him to speak.

All attention was on him, asking him about his paranormal experience.

"Tell us, tell us! We don't believe you."

Some of the portraits of long-forgotten ancestors rattled loudly on the wall, as the door was being closed.

He turned to them and said:

"I actually know a ghost.

I know him very well. He is my friend, a dear one.

His name is Charlie."

First Chapter

October 1995
Tuesday October 29th - morning
Mark

HE WOKE UP SUDDENLY. The early morning daylight was streaming into the room at full blast, it felt warm and lovely.

He didn't know where he was. The room was covered in beautiful yellow tapestries, where flowers were blooming, surrounded by green touches of spring foliage. To his left were white wooden windows that were framed by matching curtains.

He was on the bed, a huge one with a dark wood canopy, resting on the soft, yellow bedding.

He was still definitely in the house, in the hotel.

But this was not his room.

He had just woken up and was sitting upright on the bed.

He was lying on the covers, which were still neat and pressed. Fully dressed, but he had been asleep.

His head hurt. But how did he get here? He didn't remember.

It was quiet all around. He must get back to his own room.

Even though there was no-one there, he crept quietly across the room. The room remained still. He put on his shoes, slowly opened the creaking door, and looked out into the main hallway.

He recognised that he was on the first floor — on his floor — thanks to the windows in the room and in the hallway, which showcased the wonderful gardens spread out below.

But the door to this room opened onto an entirely different wing of the house.

The great staircase heading downstairs, with its vast balustrades running all around it, was right ahead of him. He must walk around the landing, back to his own corridor and head to his room. *Hopefully unseen.*

His head was still throbbing. Confusion was setting in.

Slowly but surely…he had no answers.

The hallway was complete empty, and everyone seemed to be asleep. He couldn't remember anything about the last few hours. The same experience had happened to him yesterday evening. How could this be happening to him again? What was happening to him?

He had no explanation whatsoever.

The weekend was just beginning. And the event would continue the whole of the next week.

It was supposed to be fun and lively.

He got back to his room.

Everything seemed to be in order. Just as he had left it.

The balcony doors were just slightly open, with the cold morning air rushing in, in spite of the sun. He closed them tight.

He inspected the room more closely. Nothing seemed to be missing. Then he looked at himself, and he seemed to be wearing the same clothes as yesterday.

A simple evening pants and sports jacket.

His party friends would be expecting him downstairs soon.

They mustn't be able to tell what a state he was in, he was starting to get panicky... He must get changed and dressed in fresh clothes.

He went to the bathroom, he needed to look as though nothing had happened to him.

Who was going to help him, anyway? He was confused, and all alone.

His room was a suite, nice and spacious. It was in the new section of the house. It had a more contemporary feel, with a comfortable wooden-framed bed, and adjoining the bedroom was an equally large living room with a door on the far side that led to a private balcony overlooking the gardens. He hadn't been out there yet. Hadn't had the time.

The view from the bedroom was of *the huge garden surrounding the property*, all the way down to the lawn and to a walled garden on the left of the house, where the cooks from the restaurant gathered most of their ingredients, *fresh every day*.

Though it was not visible from his windows, the hotel and its open lawn was set in the middle of a tranquil wooded area, which descended to the nearby beach and Ireland's idyllic, wild Atlantic coastline.

He took a look outside for one last time, trying to remember last night — but he just couldn't.

This will have to do for now. He gave up staring outside, returned to his room, and headed downstairs to join the others. Hoping they didn't have too many questions.

He got to the stairs. The heavy wooden staircase was one of the most attractive features of the house. Its heavy carpeting with a flower motif was soft under his shoes. *The house itself seemed to have been there forever.*

Ratmulen House Hotel was built as a manor house for a family in the 1820s, but since then it had been refurbished and remodelled several times. It had been enlarged, with new wings added, but it still kept its olde-worlde charm. During the last couple of decades, it had served as a hotel. *Handpicked antiques*, some of them dating back hundreds of years, were cared for with pride by the house staff, and *they adorned the halls, the foyer, the drawing room, the fireplaces and bookshelves.*

Mark was here with a couple of friends and acquaintances from work, celebrating of course. The idea was to get out of the city to this magical place in the countryside, to step away from their daily lives, into a more tranquil setting just a few minutes away from sandy beaches.

The group was made up of young women and men. The prettiest girls included some who already been *his lovers,* and some that just might become so, while the rest of them were his friends, enemies, or rivals... *Much like any similar gathering of people.*

He was glad he was invited, that was enough for him. *This is where he needed to be!*

So he didn't ask many questions.

Walking down to reception, a casual observer would have remarked on his handsome features, accentuated in the early morning light that was streaming in from the high windows.

The serious man behind the front desk of the reception of the Ratmulen House Hotel, straightened his tie, and watched Mark with great expectation and concern, "Excuse me, sir, Mr. Mark, the police are here. As you requested."

Mark's beautiful large eyes opened up in surprise. "The police. For me?"

"Yes, sir." He lowered his voice, "The gentlemen from the police are here. *As you requested*," he said discreetly. His voice remained respectful.

Mark took a step closer and leaned over the cold green marble of the reception counter.

"*About the robbery in your room,*" the older man continued, calmly and patiently. He leaned a bit closer. "The one you reported yesterday evening, sir," he said in a half whisper.

Mark was listening intently, his mouth slightly open.

"You found your door was wide open, the door onto the balcony...you thought that someone had got in. Sir, have you had the time to check whether anything is missing?"

Mark nodded slightly. He had no recollection of this at all.

All that he could remember was yesterday, after dinner... and then it stopped. He had talked to the reception *later?* And *someone had gotten into his room.* The doors were open, how could that be?

The police had only arrived here now... And where was he the whole night? Mark was looking slightly confused, he shook his head and could find nothing to say.

She was standing near the entrance to the drawing room, her back leaning leisurely against the wall. Her name was Margaret. Black eyes, *a half-smile on her lips*, a narrow look between her lashes. *He must not notice her.*

Not now. He fought to keep his attention on the receptionist. They mustn't know, if they hadn't noticed already, that something was up. He somehow knew that this was important. For him.

The receptionist was waiting, patiently.

"Would you like to speak to the officer now?"

"Yes, please," Mark said decisively. He was finally awake. "Please."

The receptionist, adjusted his glasses, went around the desk and motioned upstairs, back toward the staircase.

Mark didn't turn towards her again. A light perspiration appeared on his forehead.

There will be plenty of time for that – *for her* – later. *Plenty of time.*

"Follow me, please. I think he is already upstairs."

Mark obliged and followed the receptionist up the stairs. They entered his room on the first floor. The birds outside were singing to welcome what looked like quite a lovely morning.

Everything else was quiet, even the police sergeant.

All was calm. The receptionist waited outside.

Mark and the sergeant checked the balcony door handle and lock. They checked the lock on the door to the hallway.

Had he locked it properly? He couldn't remember.

It would have been quite possible for someone to get inside from the iron balcony, climbing the stairs leading up here from the garden. The stairs had not been used for a long time and were now overgrown with decorative vegetation, making them almost inaccessible.

The officer checked – yes, it did look like the vegetation had been disturbed, not so long ago.

It was possible that a burglar had gone into his room looking for valuables.

But I think it unlikely, the sergeant said.

"This is a very safe place and a quiet part of the countryside. We do believe you, though, that something has happened. Has anything gone missing? Anything of value?"

Not that Mark recollected.

"Just the feeling in the room, and the fact that the cushions have been moved about. *A strange feeling in the room,*" Mark added, but he just saw this now, when looking around the room.

The policeman noted it.

11

Mark blushed.

"And during the day, before you reported the incident to Reception after dinner, you were where?"

"I was out and about with friends. I wasn't in my room."

"Please be careful when leaving your room and make the proper safety precautions... But I don't believe you're in any danger."

The receptionist, who was still lingering in the house hallway, now looked in through the open door to Mark's room. "And during the night?" the policeman said.

"Nothing," Mark said quickly.

He didn't admit to them that not only didn't he remember reporting it or even finding his room in the state they were talking about - he couldn't remember any of it. The policeman looked up and raised his eyebrows, but he said nothing more.

This whole thing was starting to get *exhausting*.

Mark just sighed in exasperation.

"Sir, would you like to change rooms? The hotel would be glad to accommodate you in any way."

"*No. No!*" Mark said rather abruptly, now standing facing the hallway with them.

I need to stay... He didn't even know why he was so sure.

"I will stay in this room," he finished. "It is all right, gentlemen. Thank you."

They shook hands politely. "If anything is needed, do please just ask."

The policeman checked the lock on the door once again: it went *click-clack*...it was working, and so they both left. Mark was relieved.

The rooms were empty. *He took a deep breath of air.*

The men had been gone for a while now, and he was alone in his room.

But the expected sense of relief did not arrive. Instead, he felt this *pressure in his head*, and a headache coming on again. *A slight ringing in his ears.*

He pressed his hands to his face, slowly.

He hadn't got much sleep last night, it seemed. That was *what* he was feeling, this sudden sickness. He would lie down now and take a nap for a little bit.

Second Chapter

Tuesday 29th, Late morning
Mark

MARK WOKE UP A BIT LATER.

He was feeling energised, *finally*.

Shone his shoes, carefully. There was another pair that were dirty, as if from *outside,* but he left those in the corner – they were the ones he was wearing when he woke up this morning. He checked the jacket he had just put on, dusted it down, and combed his hair in the mirror.

He went out.

The week-long stay at the country estate had started only a couple of days ago, and he planned to make the most of it.

As did everyone, from the very young, spoiled, rich company he was with, he was sure of that!

All the girls and boys with their well-off parents close at hand, and a great affinity for partying. Not that *his* situation was like that... but he could get behind such a fun company!

And an environment where *he* just felt good, he was *sure* of that.

He stepped outside in front of the manor with his shiny new shoes onto the white gravel pathway. The cold, almost November wind was blowing onto the back walls of the house. So here in the front of the manor they were protected and it was quite *lovely*. The sun shone, now high up in the sky, with no clouds in sight. He looked up.

But this will change soon for sure, in the matter of a couple of minutes possibly.

That was a certainty here, so why not make the most of it now? *The amazingly tricky and never-ending Irish weather.*

His company was already there. They waved him over, excitedly.

"There you are, *Mark*," the girls shouted, accusingly.

"We have been missing you!" one of them added playfully.

He took a few quick decisive steps towards them.

Mark smiled at the other guests, rewarding them for all the attention. A loose strand of honey brown hair fell onto his face.

Describing him was as if listening to a *long-lost* song... Every tone, every melody playing in your body so familiar, yet so lost in time. The face white pale, a shining complexion with big brown eyes that would never miss even one of your moves. They are electric, deep when looking at you. The coloring of his hair, as if a warm dark chestnut, with what seemed to be disobedient waves, of strands falling over his eyes, which in fact were meticulously styled. Reminding you of stepping into a painting of a *long-lost* classical painter, the shadow and light, the dark and magnificent glimmer...set on a background of calmly falling autumn leaves turning just the color of his hair and the lighter shade present in his eyes.

Lashes long, almost lady–like. Flickering.

But if his gaze looks away from you, into the distance, suddenly there is such an indifference present. You could feel it all leaving you, his attention, throwing you into… the cold dark.

As if off a cliff, viewing the sharp edges which seemed once so sweet, while still enjoying the beautiful sight from seconds ago, fearing the uncompromising fall from the heights.

A beautiful deep memorable voice – *like honey almost.*

Wide cheeks, like a prince.

"Where have you been?" added another of the girls reproachingly.

Mark smiled at them for all the attention.

They were sitting at a table on the vast lawn in front of the hotel.

Further on stood the still and majestic trees of the local forest, leading gradually onto the dunes and into the sea. The opulent patio was decked out with iron chairs and tables, proofed against the imminent rain. It was a small space in front of the hotel, where you could get some coffee and some snacks. The rest of the tables were yet empty, it was still early.

When he joined the company, they were already jolly.

Out of the girls, there was the birthday girl and hostess, Patricia, who was joined by Margaret, Emmy and one girl he didn't know (or hadn't paid much attention to), then a few of the guys.

The remaining guests were by the ocean, he was told. They would join them later.

The waitress brought him a coffee with a shot of Irish whiskey. *Just what he needed.*

If they were in luck, they could probably see this sunshine for about ten more minutes. Then the drizzle would probably come again. Why not enjoy it?

The new girl, the one he didn't know, smiled at him, and as she leaned over, she brushed his knee with her hand. *He was definitely aware of it.* And he was fine with it. It happened to him a lot recently. His good looks and charm got him far. Far enough to score an invitation to this place! So...*why should they not get him even further?*

He found that he was able to put yesterday's and this morning's events out of his mind and enjoy the company.

One of the guys handed him a whole bottle of Jameson under the table, with a wink, "Just in case, for later..." he laughed. "We must keep healthy!"

It was true, in changeable weather such as this, all you could do was keep on drinking.

The guys at the party were nice to him as well, sometimes he thought *too* nice, so he got on with them rather easily. Some of them he knew better, some of them not at all... anyhow he decided not to get mixed up with them, because it could be a slippery slope. He decided just to stick with fun with the girls, that was easy for him.

They had been here for a couple of days, with about four more nights to go.

He must stay on the good side of everybody during that time.

So, he must keep his options open.

Be careful. Even while flirting.

But that was not an easy quest... He got all of their attention, now he must try to keep it.

He wasn't much of a talker, not really. But here, between all these people, he had to be. He had to try. Be what they wanted him to *be*, what was expected from him. Be like them. Because...in a simple way this is it is done. How it is. It didn't really matter, where he was from, what he was like. *Only if he complied.*

To became a part of it all, the well-oiled machine. Maybe stand up a little, with some extraordinary talent of his. He *smirked to himself:* sure. But not too much. Just the right amount.

Just to make the company shine.

Oh, how he hated people. Hated them all.

If it was up to him, he would be somewhere in a caravan on the sea shore, just parked. *Looking at the sunrise... alone.* And maybe, pretty sure - he might be ending like that soon enough.

If he doesn't try hard enough, give his effort. *This weekend.* To be like that.

Smile. Enjoy life. Charm. All the people around him.

He had his looks. And is what brought him around to people in the first place. *Made them more accessible and open to him thanks to that. But that was about it, the only advantage of it.* So, he learned to use it for his own benefit. And to combine it with a projection of a person who was likable, *care-free even. A hands on – hands off lover.*

But what was he really even like? ...He didn't even know.

No family to fall back to. Not money to fall onto.

To keep his back and held out a helping hand. Give him a boost of confidence.

When he needed it.

He felt this was his chance in life. So young, being 24 years old, to be thinking like he was.

He just didn't have the energy. He felt weak, tired. So alone.

Like there would be nothing else waiting for him. In life.

Where to go - where to succeed. Which direction to take.

But the others mustn't see him like that. *Must not see how sad he was. How angry he as.*

He must, just must keep his face on.

What he probably needed, for himself, was calm and stability. And maybe someone to care for him. *Make him feel he was – enough. See him as he was: as he is.*

Someone who was in his corner; like this was a boxing ring.

But he hadn't felt the strength to fight, not anymore. *His heart – broken in.*

Inwards – from the *many, many* things that had come before. Even maybe in his teenage years.

Or was it really mended – or even properly put together, in the first place?

But for now... there is just this.

He loves his job, he is good at it. *So why not succeed in that?*

But in a profession like this it wasn't sure you will keep your position; it was very volatile, very competitive... and in the end based on personal relationships!

He really liked every part of it. The scouting of the new property, diving into the project. The sales, surveys, decision making, all this everywhere around and throughout the country. Amazing.

When one is trying to move forward - they would say: "Don't take the money."

But he would, would take the money! He could see himself like that.

Driving a low smooth, midnight silver car: firmly on the road, the steering wheel in his hands.

So here he was. This weekend, at this glorious historical mansion, whose charm was not lost on him. Trying to be nice to people, but to stay closed, so, they wouldn't see. Not to embarrassed himself, in any way. Not show weakness.

When people talked to him, he tried to feel less. Not to feel that much, like he usually does. People just would not understand. *This was it.*

He was here at the invitation of the boss's daughter, the birthday girl. The hostess, no less. She liked him. Staying in a great room, with an incredible view. She invited him to come. But there were no sparks there, just friendly. And that is the way it will stay.

They had a nice relationship. Why mess with that? And she had other interest here *indeed.*

That is what Mark would not do: go after the bosses' daughter. That he won't, like all the other suckers-ups here! All of them in a way.

He thought she just didn't deserve that. If that was a way he didn't feel.

But shaking hands with the father, that he could do! That sounded interesting.

Being appreciated for who he is. *How he is.* That was a thing that he wanted. A thing he *would go for.*

A *firm handshake.* Approving smile. Appreciation from the Big Man.

Himself smiling modestly but surely looking into his eyes. So, he felt it.

When he finally found a moment to relax, to forget about the strange events - that he actually could not remember - *this was one of the first questions for him, from his friends:*

"So, tell us Mark…who was that lovely lady we saw you running around with?"

The day looked so hopeful and nice; but he thought, *this* is going to be the last of *him.*

It seems the evening events and beyond were to come back to haunt him, *to be heard of again.*

Even sooner and in a way he did not expect. People occasionally came up to him during the whole day and mentioned: something he couldn't recall talking to them about, at all! *...about the dinner they had that night, what drinks they had...something that he promised he will do or be a part of today.* The days here were short... but evenings well, seemed very long *indeed.*

He just shrugged the answer off, with no concrete reaction.

They will put it down to heavy drinking. No bother.

He hoped. That is what was expected. He smiled to himself:

If he was going through something, there was no-one here he wanted to talk to about it.

The girls were admiring him, lots of giggling going on, what more could he ask for?

Later on, the sun was setting quickly again, a lot earlier since it was almost winter time, the end of October. It got dark almost before four o'clock - you could feel the dusk coming on.

The fun in the sun was over, at least for today.

Soon the whole house and grounds would be beneath a curtain of darkness that would envelop them.

His company thought nothing of his behaviour: they remained as cheerful as ever.

They sat around the comfortable drawing rooms, near the flaming fireplaces, before dinner.

Whoever was bored could pick up a deck of cards, challenge someone to a chess game, or take a look at some of the books in the nearby library. All the leatherbound books looked well-worn, but probably if you searched through them, you could find a nice detective story to read. "Or a ghost story...!", one of the girls laughed.

"Let's not read, let's talk!" That is what they did... most of the time.

Such gossips they all were.

Then, just shortly before dinner time, the birthday girl decided they, *the girls*, should go upstairs and change. *To get all pretty,* she said. Ready for the evening festivities. The girls were giddy, it seemed they loved dressing up. But Mark suddenly felt a dread come over him, as if he was not so sure of himself and the upcoming night anymore. The feeling from the earlier events came rushing back. The calm he had felt during the afternoon seemed to be fleeting.

"*Don't panic*" he said to himself. The events of last night, the dinner before that – served at six o'clock in the main dining room – he did not remember any of it.

But that doesn't mean anything. As he went to his room to change his clothes, he found nothing was amiss there, and thought to himself:

...This is going to be a nice evening.

Third Chapter

IT WAS MORNING AGAIN. He woke up with a jolt, upright in the bed.

The bed was comfortable and warm. He felt entirely different.

His whole body ached.

He looked down. He was in his evening clothes. Underneath the covers.

Everything seemed to be in place, only… the trouble was: the morning sunshine coming in through the windows.

Windows in a room he did not recognise.

By the looks of the light, it was about 9 o'clock.

It had happened again.

He got out of the bed with a gasp. It was a difficult task.

He felt his body starting to shake all over. As if the simple act of getting up was too much for it to bear. His feet were bare. His legs muddy. His pants – gone.

He had never seen this room before. Was he here for the first night when this happened? He looked back at the bed. It was slept in alright. The sheets were crumpled, the pillows disarranged, the duvet all over the place. As if there had been a fight here, really.

Not again! A small hiss came out of his throat.

He was not himself, that was for sure. *He smashed his hand into the pillow. Aargh!*

That gave him no answer.

There must be some explanation for this. No comprehension. There must be an end to this, for sure… he hoped. His pants and jacket looked like they had been *soaked*, he found them lying on the floor, though otherwise in good condition. Now they were dry again.

He must have been outside.

Suddenly he thought he caught a whiff of a sweet scent in the air.

Then it was gone.

All he could smell now were his dirty clothes.

With the sea air, and the moss and seaweed.

Who will help him?

He must get on and find his way back into his own room. Looking like this – looking like hell.

He put himself together.

To throw down some breakfast.

Ironically, he was too early, there was nobody in the dining room yet, now.

He was seated at one of the tables.

He could not go back *to his room*, he felt the adrenaline rushing through his body.

Last night events forgotten, again. Like that, all of it.

He almost felt like laughing. Felt a wave of hysteria coming over him. When he really started, whilst being alone, the waiter looked at him *strangely*.

He stopped. He must be more careful.

Not let it get to him… The cup of good strong coffee, few beans, will make him feel better. A bit of food, stronger.

He needed to think, calmly, let the calm pass over him – then he would remember the events of last night, surely? Nothing came to him. *He tried.* Just him being in his room yesterday, he could picture it, putting on his evening clothes. Shaving, who knows even why.

The same clothes that he now found soaked, laying on the floor of a strange, a lot smaller, hotel room in the manor.

The tapestries were dark, this time.

Dark red, like wine.

He was not alone. He could feel it.

For a moment a shadow of a memory came rushing by.
Then it was gone.

He touched his cheeks, he was cleanly shaven, his face soft. Again, that whiff of a scent.

Was it a cream, an aftershave, a perfume? He could *not* tell. The warm food tasted good.

He was starting to feel himself again.

Good that he hadn't met anybody from his company, not just yet.

A wave of guests started coming into the room, mainly other guests who were staying at the manor. *Steady.*

He was determined to act as if almost nothing had happened.

He noticed several from his own party were drifting in as well. It was nearing 10 o'clock. They were yawning, stretching, laughing quietly. The girls were dressed in light, loose clothes, too light for this kind of weather. He got up quickly, so he didn't have to wave and smile and say *hello*. He just didn't feel up to it. He left the dining room hastily, through a door on the opposite side of the hall, leading to the French doors opening at the back, into the gardens.

He let out a big sigh. He was looking outside, standing in front of the glass windows of this exit, he was alone here. Now, it was a dark morning outside. Usually, this would have looked so romantic to him, after all the sun. Even as if it was threatening to rain.

Or had it been raining through the night? *He wished he knew.*

How was he going to make it through today?

He turned back inside through a different corridor, skipping the dining area, and went into the library and sat at one of the fireplaces. The girls were merry, again. They leaned closer to him.

"So, tell us Mark... who is the girl we have seen you with?"

Mark was astonished.

"Tell us Mark." said another one, "*Who is she?* Are you in love?" she added playfully.

They were giggling again.

"What are you talking about?" he said.

"Well, we saw you…" now the birthday girl cut in, in a more serious tone, "…with this lady. In the fields. Close to the hotel. You were probably going to the beach."

"How very romantic!" the first girl screamed into his ear.

"Well, who is she… ? Is she local?"

Now was a good time, Mark knew, *to appear mysterious.* He put on his best enigmatic, half smile.

"If you won't tell us, don't then," the birthday girl added in her deep baritone voice.

This girl, she had more sense to her, Mark was thinking. She had invited him after all. He liked her. But not in the same way as Margaret. She entered the room and was now getting closer to the table. *She made his blood really boil.*

A dark, raven-haired beauty, one would call her.

She definitely knew how to play hard to get.

"She was very beautiful," the first girl added.

Margaret was looking on, in their direction, listening to what was going on.

Mark just nodded absently. Looking at the table beneath his fingers. He felt an involuntary shiver down his spine. Who were they talking about? Or were they just leading him on… was this a big joke?

He remembered no such woman.

He was definitely not in love.

While thinking these thoughts he was looking at Margaret, mesmerised. She was still standing up:

"*Who* are you talking about?"

"Ah, well. Mark is in love..." the first girl added conspiratorial way.

"Didn't you see her?" the second girl chipped in, "On the field, near the woods with him, before dusk."

Margaret sat down next to them: "I didn't see anything like that."

Mark was relieved.

So maybe they were really making fun of him.

Was he in the woods before dusk, in his best clothes and in love? It was true that his clothes were wet when he woke. He was suddenly not so sure anymore.

His thoughts were interrupted as the first girl returned to the conversation, having been distracted by something else for a while: "Wait - couldn't she be the one that broke into your room and stole your things?"

"*Nothing was stolen,*" Mark felt the need to clarify, and he said emphatically, "Just someone got into the room." Good, they know this already...

Could what they were saying – could it really mean something? He was hopeful, it might.

"We must contact the police and tell them!" one of other girls said, now more alarmed.

The birthday girl had moved a while ago to a different table, socialising. She was the butterfly of the event after all.

"But who is she? *What does she look like?* Could you describe her to the police?"

The girls were talking amongst themselves: they were lively now, talking over each other.

They just left Mark staring vacantly out of the window. One of them was saying:

"Now really, I couldn't. I didn't see her face. *Just her clothes, really fancy ones, I'd say.*"

"Could she be our little burglar? Should we be terrified?" Margaret added in a sly voice, staring at him as he turned to face her, and now she yawned.

"Really, Mark, if you want to make something of it, you should tell the police who she is. And all about her," said the first of the girls in a worried but engaged tone. She looked him in the eye, unwavering.

This was Mark's cue to leave, he knew that.

This made him uneasy. He would get himself into trouble… He didn't say anything, making his way to leave, looking pale. As he made his way out of the chair and from the table, the second girl shouted, "Crazy in love, he is!" And they all giggled.

He stumbled out the drawing room into the hall, propping himself against one of the columns next to the doorway, his knees shaking.

What was happening to him was definitely not normal.

Fourth Chapter

Wednesday 30th, Late afternoon
Sebastian

THE LAST RAYS OF SUNLIGHT WERE FALLING ON THE RECEPTION DESK, A FEW METERS FROM THE MAIN ENTRANCE DOOR.

The door was now closed but unlocked for visitors and guests to wander in and out, as the cold was quickly setting outside for the upcoming night.

The reception staff, a girl and an older gentleman, switched on all the lights *one by one*. Lamp stands, chandeliers. Even with *all* of the lights on, the lighting of the place was *romantic and peaceful*. The girl shivered slightly. They put on the *heating* as well.

It seemed like it was going to be a slow night tonight.

The dinner was beginning at six sharp, so still an hour away.

No wonder it was cold, it was going to be November soon, and that is not such a nice month to be by the Atlantic Coast.

They were setting the tables now, giving finishing touches to the place settings.

The biggest party they had at the moment in the hotel, a party of twenty youngish people had reserved the largest table in the *main dining hall*.

It was a birthday party of sorts, which spanned the entire week. Really a group of people from the city, they will be here through the end of November until *after the All Souls Eve.*

Fine-looking people, *the reception girl made this observation*, who sure knew how to have fun *indeed.* As if almost this setting of their old Georgian style manor was a bit *too classical* for them, the girl smirked a bit.

But they had class: that was for sure.

The hotel tried the best to accommodate them during the stay, for the fun during the day, and their evening entertainment.

There is going to be a big costume party for them tomorrow, with a twenties theme: catered by the hotel. The guests will have fancy dress costumes, there will be music, champagne bottles by the dozen... *The reception girl was quite excited just thinking about it.* Too bad the next day is her night off though.

Into these calm thoughts came a sudden interruption.

The front door burst open.

The receptionist staff lifted their heads up.

The cold winds were coming in from outside at a ghastly speed.

A few leaves were caught in spirals and came in with a drizzle of rain.

In the doorway was standing a youngish man.

Dressed kind of odd.

34

The reception girl noticed it was not just the clothes itself, but the way he was rather disheveled. As if the outside elements did a number on him.

But that was not where the drama ended. *On the contrary.*

What came out of him, when he spoke. There was a great sense of urgency to him:

"*I have been called here by the spirits.* "

The receptionists both rolled their eyes.

The young man continued:

"*I have been called here to this place.*

Someone is in danger. In danger from the dark forces from the woods. "

The storm outside was starting to grow in its intensity. It felt like thunder was coming.

"If I do not intervene there is great peril.

Someone has got inside, infiltrated this house.

I have been summoned here, I have sensed it, they need my help!

I am a clairvoyant.

I had a vision.

I have experience in these matters, I offer my help. "

He looked up at them now. *The cold blue eyes of the strange visitor have not blinked once.*

But girls standing nearby, just exiting one of the drawing rooms with fireplaces on the left, were left mesmerized. Hand on their mouths, and on each other's bare arms, they giggled merrily.

"This is so great, so exciting! " they exclaimed.

They probably thought it was all part of the festivities program, a fun game.

Or even if not.

They did not feel the cold on their skin, in their skimpy little dresses - so exhilarated they were!

"Are you for real? "

Now the stranger blinked. Not sure what to make of it.

He was getting used to his surroundings. He straightened his turned-up collar.

Just when the receptionist was about to proclaim something, thrown him out probably. *What a joke!* The girls gathered around him.

The visitor smiled a little, a soft smile. They invited him for dinner.

To be with them this evening.

They have to hear more!

Oh, well, if they want him, *thought the receptionist*, and decided not to interfere. Maybe he was indeed *a part of the celebrations* after all. And he put it out of his head.

The eerie visitor. With such a strange premonition.

He was now their guest for dinner at the manor.

Fifth Chapter

MARK WAS WATCHING THIS FROM UP ABOVE. He was terrified, and felt the fear in his bones.

He was standing overlooking the reception area, on the manor's first floor landing, where his room was. He saw the whole scene. Heard every word the visitor had said.

Sank right into his soul.

He just knew, *knew*, this was about him.

He didn't ask for this.

He wasn't...looking for this.

He saw how the girls fluttered around him, inviting him to dinner.

Mark watched the whole scene, but hidden, unseen.

Steadying himself against the railings. *Holding on tightly.*

Catching his breath.

Then he carefully, not to be noticed, went down the corridor back to his room.

He shut himself inside.

He closed the door behind him tightly.

Sixth Chapter

THE DINNER BEGAN.

All was just beautiful around them, the aromas and sounds.

Sebastian was seated in among the girls. *Comfortably,* he must say.

They were easy-going...with their *soft silk dresses, and glowing skin.*

The fun was in full swing around him.

The food was warming and tasty. People called to one another across the table, and laughter came and went in waves. No-one was surprised by his presence. They took him as a matter of fact. *Greeted him as a part of their company.*

Sebastian was accustomed to being on his own.

A *lone wolf* you might call him. That was how he liked it. *Being his own man.* Not relying on anyone else too much...he did his research and travelled the country.

But there wasn't anyone he felt really close to.

He followed his gut, his intuition, and the wind... And still stayed part of civilised society.

It was his research that had brought him here, tonight.

To this easy flowing company. Pretty girls, champagne: he didn't mind...

Despite the lively goings on, the food and the drinks, Sebastian still had a lot of time to look around at the other guests.

But he couldn't find what he came looking for. *Why, why here?* He just had no clue.

The dining room was huge, in a very open, spacious part of the hotel ground floor.

Their party was seated around a large table near the bar and the kitchen, but they were not the only occupants of the dining room: there were a few other guests. But they definitely held the main focus of the waiting staff.

Another whiskey, please!

Bring *a whole bottle, to save time...*

The other "innocent" guests of the manor were soberly observing the party. Outside, beyond the windows, it had long since turned dark. The whole dining hall was nicely lit, even now with the splashes of rain outside. They were not sitting by the windows, more in the centre of the room. And their party was warm enough – and getting warmer...

No, don't drink water! Don't drink that!

No one asked for any details about the exact reason behind Sebastian's presence.

He was just a part of the entertainment for them.

One of the girls told him, that the *whole week event* was a roaring twenties theme here. *If that is even a thing, Sebastian raised an eyebrow...* That is the wish of their hostess.

This is just a dinner; the main event will be tomorrow. A ball of sorts, with dancing, live music, the whole works.

They are from the city. Where is he from?

They are laughing to his curt answers.

No! He dressed just so, appropriately; the dinner jacket he is wearing now will do.

He is just a doll.

He was really cute, the ladies *whispered*. As they watched him, they would see:

Sebastian's hair was in a short, but elegant, cut and it was the colour of wet hay.

His eyes twinkled warmly, but on close inspection they seemed to change from a surprisingly light green to the palest blue that shone like moonlight. His step was light when coming in, the touch of his arm *was gentle...*his hand just touching the small of your back and leading you forward, in such a way as you almost couldn't feel it. And yet *his embrace didn't give off any warmth*, even though he seemed like a warm person...

His clothes were usually slightly old fashioned, greyish blue and grass green shades that seemed to reflect in his eyes. Sebastian's lips formed a tight line and gave him rather a stern look, but he was still attractive. *His appearance was rather like snow falling onto the dark bark rooftop of a winter cabin, with a warming fire burning brightly inside.*

But he saw himself truly as a lone wolf.

Well, but *he could put on the charm*, when he wanted to. But mostly he kept to himself. He was his own best company.

But perhaps that was about to change.

The one advantage of the place where they were seated was that Sebastian had a clear view of the entrance area: who was coming...who was going.

He kept watching carefully, to see whether there was anything he might have missed. He took in everything around him, and he saw that the house he was in was truly glorious.

Lots of wooden ornaments, paintings...class.

He really liked his room as well. The room which he took and where he had left his things for the night. The place had history for sure.

The dining hall where they were now was a bit more sober, but it continued with the theme of *sweetly-scented rooms* and plush velvets of the seats and sofas, surrounding the main reception, *with the small fireplaces softly burning.*

Now he saw it.

There was a new guest in the entrance door.

He was a bit late.

He was looking around the room and people unsurely, a bit shyly even.

He had nice locks of hazel hair, coming in short waves.

A black and white suit, quite precise.

The others waived at him to come to the table; he smiled finally and signalled back.

His feet and legs were soaking wet... as if covered in a mossy green cover. But no one else could see this but him, Sebastian. Not maybe even the new gentleman himself. As if he had been marked...in a spiritual world sense. But what did that mean?

It was all over his calves when he moved.

Water dripping from the new guest as he walked towards them, hands in his pockest, only no-one seemed to notice it. Sebastian could feel an uneasiness coming over him.

What he was seeing he could not quite place. What an odd sensation.

Sebastian is now surprised and in shock. *Is he the only one that is seeing it?*

The grass dew or sea water dripping, moss, maybe even seaweed, caught around the ankles of the other man. That must be so.

This is *what* he came looking for. *He* is what is he is looking for, more precisely. The new guest.

But the party is all laughing now at something else: their attention is elsewhere.

Sebastian is looking around and still nobody is saying anything, their new guest is placed to sit not that far away from him, still smiling quite shyly, aimlessly.

As if he was uncomfortable. Now he is looking at his empty plate, at his hands.

But never at Sebastian.

He never meets his eye. The new gentleman never once lifts his eyes from the nice whimsical glass of champagne on ice he has now got in his grasp, to meet Sebastian's.

The evening is moving on and the ladies get him quite engaged, so he is not shy, not anymore. He is talking to them, but still rather calmly and with reserve.

Looking at them deeply with his Bambi eyes, they are *wriggling with pleasure.*

But you could still feel the uneasiness and heaviness around him.

It struck Sebastian as odd that this new guest never once asked who he even was. Nor looked in his direction. He was sat across from Sebastian at the head of the L-shaped table. Looking first to his right and to his left at girls who were sitting next to him, engaging him now in lively conversation.

It was completely natural the way they were seated that Sebastian could look over in his direction, and thus watch him, without appearing overly curious. But he never looked back at him.

Not once.

It was as if he already knew who he was.

Never once raising a question who Sebastian is. Never once looking into his direction.

The gentleman who caught Sebastian's attention sees a sudden stranger for a guest: yet he is not curious.

As if he already knew who he was.

It was soon clear to him that only *he* had seen the water and the foliage.

Not that he was surprised.

He expected something like that, something out of the ordinary to reach out for him, while looking at all the guests here. Some sign, something that was sent just for him. The reason he felt he must be here. The feeling of danger came over him like waves crashing on the beach nearby in the dead of the darkness.

When he looked back at him new gentleman, *he was looking.*

He was looking back at him now, with a strangely calm look, still shy. As if frightened, bashful, not saying anything.

But still he had not uttered one word in Sebastian's direction. As the evening moved on, the new guest relaxed a bit.

As did Sebastian. The food was nice, the company good.

The people called him "Mark". So that was probably his name.

Seventh Chapter

Later on Sebastian caught up with him on the first floor landing, above the reception.

Mark was decisive but discreet, pulled him aside; he was firm and intense towards him.

He started talking to Sebastian immediately. He was friendly now, but still quite tense:

"I am the one you are looking for. It's me.

I am the reason you are here."

He says to him that his name is Mark. That he needs to talk to him. That he is happy that he came. He calls him to his bedroom.

This early in their relationship? This is what Sebastian was waiting for, not wanting to make the first move at dinner. Not to spook him out, of course…

Yet Sebastian smirks. And at that moment he is a bit indecisive, hesitating. Thinking to himself: *this Mark seems quite the ladies' man and what not. With all the nice ladies whirling around Mark tonight.. He can bet he won't get into the good graces of his kind hostesses, with this step right now!*

But what does he care: this is probably indeed why he came here, what for.

Mark pulls him closer right now: "You got to help."

"*Yes. Okay, sure.*"

Mark is leading the way to his room. He does not ask Sebastian any personal questions, not one *single* bit. He doesn't seem to interested *who he is and where he came from tonight.*

They don't go past Sebastian single bedroom, which he took for the night. That is on the floor below them.

Cozy, but quite roomy, that is where he had left his things.

Where he was planning on spending the night.

Mark leads him into his room, which it is surprisingly spacious, a suite in fact. Sebastian follows him inside. It has an entrance foyer which leads to the bedroom, a glorious king-size bed overlooking the large old-style glazed windows to the garden, with what must be a magnificent view during the day. A precise wooden carving is on the elaborate bedhead, and there is a heavy wooden closet on the right-hand wall.

This all then leads to an open living room to the left. With a few sofas, armchairs and tables. *What comfort.* Sebastian is still looking around. As they walk further into the room, Mark turns to him, with fright in his eyes. He goes on to tell him: "You must help me..." *He tells him what has been happening to him.*

He seats himself the sofa, keeps on talking.

The sofa is looking onto to the French doors which lead outside, onto a small iron balcony.

A few lovely paintings are hanging on the walls. *A small bar on the far side.*

"And you are sure you are not sleep-walking?" Sebastian wants him to elaborate.

Sebastian continues: "In different bedrooms... And how do you know you aren't going there with someone? Are you really sure? It is possible you are influenced by the full moon, which culminates in a few days from now... I mean – if you were sleepwalking."

Mark keeps looking at him eagerly, taking a sip of water out of a heavy glass.

Offers him a glass as well. His hands are shaking, they are pale, he keeps grabbing at them.

A slight smell of cologne comes Sebastian's way... Marks eyes are darting around the room, but still at the same time he is listening to Sebastian, talking intently.

When Mark's gaze fixes upon him, Sebastian sees his eyelashes fluttering slightly around his hazel brown eyes.

"...It is possible it is influencing you. Even if you don't have previous experiences. The moon will be full in three nights. This time it actually falls exactly on the upcoming night of *All Souls Eve. That is why you are here, isn't it – to celebrate?*

It is a Super Blood Moon, its effect may be even stronger. *So you might be more influenced by this, even if you weren't before."*

Mark retorts he is not a sleepwalker, but now it may seem like it. "But how do you explain that I was capable of avoiding the stairs completely...and I didn't hurt himself, if I am actually sleepwalking? In such an unknown place to me.

And the woman I have been seen with, in the early and late evenings, walking around the grounds? Other people have been seeing me with her, outside. I don't remember anything of it, anything of a girl... Her soft blonde hair, nothing... Could I have been sleeping?"

He is nervous, shaking. Moving up and down in his chair again.

Sebastian is sure Mark is usually a different kind of man... *Definitely does not seem himself right now.* With small drops of sweat on his forehead, his oh-so white shirt is suddenly all crumpled beneath his jacket. Sebastian feels almost sorry for him.

His companion is definitely not himself, above all else.

Sebastian is hit with a sudden wave of affection towards him: the young man asking for *his* help, with no prejudice and questions towards his being whatsoever. Sebastian is sure that what he is seeing right now is not the type of man Mark usually presents himself to be.

Is he getting a glimpse now, seeing behind the curtain of the soul of another person?

"Stay here, during the night, stay with me." *What, here?*

"Spend the night. Here in this room." Mark comes up with a solution just like that. A plea:

"I will pay you. You will help me to find out what is happening to me."

He gets up and is looking around himself now.

"This is the reason you came here - after all. You will protect me.

If you really are, who you say you are, then you have some special powers, gifts, abilities... That will help, you know..." he trails off. "Or if it is only a normal thing – and I am indeed sleepwalking... at least, I will be safe. You will be here to protect me; you will keep me safe. With you."

He is right.

Yet the whole night? He is a lovely man. With some reputation, or so Sebastian thinks. Someone from the party probably saw him coming into the room with him... What the others will think, *with his reputation*, it is easy to imagine!

But Sebastian already knows he will agree.

So he does.

Eighth Chapter

MARK FALLS ASLEEP ON THE SOFA, AS IF OUT OF PURE EXHAUSTION.

Sebastian feels for him. As a puppy who needs to be protected. *He needs him.* His companion is putting his trust into him, Sebastian, so completely: that is amazing. To a stranger.

But he must stay vigilant. Must not let him down.

There is probably something at force here. *At large.* That will not be making the situation easy for him. Mark is sleeping, his head on the sofa pillow now. Sebastian is sitting comfortably in the armchair facing him. It is dark, the lights are on only as a dim shadow.

He feels something is going on.

Something is about to happen. *Soon.*

He can feel the hairs on his body being electrified slightly.

He can feel it in the air.

No time for rest or relaxation for Sebastian. *The air outside is singing to the rhythm of a sleepy wind. A cry of a lonely owl, otherwise nothing.*

From the balcony doors he hears the soft dripping of raindrops on the railings, the buzz of the faraway sea.

It is so calm now, the dead of night so that you can almost hear it.

He *feels* that it is a sign something will happen. So, he waits.

The atmosphere in the room is changing. It is charged. A pressure that is impossible to describe. *Then he hears a knock at the balcony door, knocking on glass.*

Now again. It is coming from outside.

"Charlie! Charlie...!?" a girl is gently calling out.

Softly but intensely.

He goes and opens the door to the elegant balcony: on the landing there is a woman standing. She is wearing an unusual dress: a few ruffles around her knees, then a long skirt down to her ankles.

A beautiful face, pouting lips, she is looking at something intensely through the night.

The cold air is brisk.

But you cannot feel the cold coming from her at all.

She is perfectly and fashionably put together, hair and evening wear.

If it wasn't for her being *translucent* through *her pretty ankles*, so that Sebastian can already see through them the bottom of the balcony and black ground beneath, he would believe *indeed* she is a *real person*.

The see-through almost *glass-like* slippers on her feet tell a different story to him, thought.

"Charlie?" she wants to push through, push inside. She takes one look at him, Sebastian, and it is obvious he is not the one *she is looking for*. She is not here for him.

"*Let me in ...*" she says impatiently.

So, Sebastian does, stands to the side, a little.

As if in the *moment he wasn't capable of anything else* anyhow. *Cannot control his body at all.*

She leaps inside, towards Mark, laying on the sofa in a curled-up position.

The girl sits close to him on the sofa, stroking his soft hair with her hand, being very emotional. *It is all happening so fast.* She is soothing him, puts his head and pillow on her lap, still stroking him. In the dark.

Sweetly whispering: "*Charlie, Charlie...*"

As if in a voice of longing...*voice of a lover.*

She is so worried almost, yet so gentle and intense. Irresistible really.

Sebastian sits down. Quickly back into his armchair, watching them.

He asks calmly: "Leave him be. Leave him be..."

She sighs. She seems so worried now, again?

But not for herself, but for the boy laying there with her. *She is making a fuss.*

Moaning again so melodramatically, throwing meaningful glances in the way of Sebastian, so that he lets them be, leaves them alone.

"He doesn't want to go with you..." Sebastian presumes that is what she wants. He says it again firmly, unshaken. Trying to get through to her, this odd vision of a girl. So that she really hears him and not just to spook her away.

Most of the time the girl seems to be faraway, in her own world though.

But now she replies to his pleading:

"On no..." she says in a sweet voice, a peculiar accent. *"But he must, I have to...* "she trails off.

She continues in a small voice, as she starts again. As if it is difficult for her to speak:

"I can't stay here. Inside. Here I will be murdered in three days ... "

She strokes Mark's face a few times, he is fast asleep, breathing deeply. And now one more time through his soft rich, hazelnut hair.

She gets up and moves towards the open window of the balcony.

Sights deeply and emotionally a few times more.

And then she disappears and is gone.

Sebastian is turning slowly towards her direction. Two fast steps in her see-through slippers towards the balcony and she is gone. She dissipates into the night ambience.

Sebastian can't even move; feeling as if there is something wrong with him.

He is still in shock, looking worriedly towards Mark, who is surprisingly asleep.

After her presence here in the room, even though she is not here anymore, there is a lingering sense of beauty and wistfulness in the air.

No wonder Mark was so charmed with her.

Sebastian gets up and closes the balcony door. He sits himself back down. He is afraid to go to sleep... But it seems to be all over, for now. He did manage to protect him, after all.

But what if she comes back again?

For him, Mark.

When he himself, Sebastian, is fast asleep. *No, he must stay awake. Watch after him.*

He must protect him, he felt this to be true to his calling. No sleep for him tonight.

Ninth Chapter

Ratmulen House, 1927

IT USED TO BE A LARGE, GLITTERING HOUSE.
The parties that they held were mostly private, but they could go on for almost a month at a time. What a fun-loving place it was.

She and her husband were renowned for being the perfect hosts. Everyone hoped to be invited, from near and very far away: it was the hottest invitation to receive.

She was notorious for waking up in different bedrooms of the mansion almost every day. She just loved it. Well, she had the whole house just for herself, hadn't she? All the rooms...just for her. Her husband built it just for her.

It had a wild side to it too.

He had built the house so that they could organise gatherings and entertainment - just like these. All within the perfect nature and serenity of the countryside, the beach with waves splashing onto the white pebbles within reach. All surrounded by such a healthy air.

The parties had been going on all day long: all night long. There was champagne and cocktails; dancing and music, and lights poured out through the windows, across the lawns and through the clear ocean air. There had been so many things to celebrate...oh so many occasions! They were always able to find an excuse: an anniversary, a birthday, *a special date. Masquerade balls were held, celebrated business successes or new ventures, you name it: they held a party for every occasion. All the people they knew gathered around them.*

All that time ago, it seemed like a lifetime.

He had hit her on the head.

He had hit her a couple of times more.

She had wanted to run away with her younger lover; to leave her older husband and start a new life.

She had been carrying out her plan, when she died.

Tenth Chapter

THE PARTY IN THE HOUSE IS STILL GOING THE NEXT DAY, ALTHOUGH EVERYBODY IS A BIT SLEEPY IN THE MORNING. It was early, when Sebastian left Mark to sleep some more. It seemed he was safe. The sun was up.

There are a few things he wants to look into now, Sebastian decides to take a deeper look at where he actually is. He takes a look out of the window as if it would help him, sees a fog rolling slowly in. The sky is not clear yet. The fog is heading in from the woods.

It all looks so simple, not exciting at all. Not even pleasant: so to speak.

He made a few calls to his local contact, to make a start on his research. To give himself a clearer picture. There was usually a lot of official documentation in the local archives regarding important properties such as this house over the years. The owners of such properties and their families usually tended to be influential and held an important position in their communities.

In any case he was pleased that he had made such good contacts among the locals. His new historical research day job took him all round this and surrounding rural areas, and he was able to meet lots of like-minded people. So, he had helpers, and they were eager to help him, now, when time was of the essence.

They were returning him the favour, because he had been so willing to help them in the past, in more ways than one... He found them open and welcoming, mainly because they shared the same passion: history. *Maybe for a different reason than him, though.*

It shouldn't be a problem to find out whether there was something of interest in the manor house's history. *Something that could even then be echoing in the well-lit, beautiful halls.*

He was so grateful he had people he could ask to help him with his research, when it was urgent. He could consult experts in local records and archivists; check magazine libraries and almanacs... There was another aspect: researchers were also the kind of people who would be eager to discover some kind of mystery. Who would really immerse themselves in it and dig into it with passion. He would take advantage of their unique talent. *Maybe finding something that remains hidden is needed.*

Many of them carried out research as a hobby as well, maybe even in their free time...but for the same purposes as Sebastian. He just saw the world in a different light. He understood what happened and might be happening even now, around them. *Time is not linear, as people assume it is. He believed; he knew. To him, time was just amazing: yes, magical.*

He is here looking for signs *that magic* really exists.

The house *itself* might hold a lot of information, with its lovely, dusty old libraries. It was possible that some of the books and archives belonging to the house were never touched. He liked to go through it personally and search as well. Question is, is it for the public to see? He will ask at the reception. But he is not sure, they may not be... cooperative.

If there is something from the days of old that holds interest for truth-seekers nowadays, it is possible that the hotel will like to keep it private. And maybe even hidden, from the casual visitor, passing through the house and enjoying it throughout the seasons. *Sounds about right.*

Luckily, the reception staff said for him to look in the library, the smaller room to the left.

And not to forget...a place as old as this, there were always stories, legends and ghost stories. *Some places have them more than others.* And of course, if events in the history call for it, this brings out a lot of amateur historians. They are great at gathering information and keeping stories alive in the community, in the way of being precise and professional...they may be lacking. He must look into it all.

So, all things considered, it had been fairly easy for him to gather information quickly about the history he needed to look into.

His aim this morning was to look into some of the unresolved mysteries in the surrounding area, as well as the manor house he was staying at right now, particularly any unsolved cases. *Or notorious ones.* He started from the date that the house was built, during the 18th century. There was a lot of work to do...so it was useful that he had free time to devote to it.

Sebastian was surprised that in a short amount of time, lots of information turned up. And among his discoveries were some surprises. He had hastily put together background to support his research. Dating early back he couldn't really find anything of interest to him that was documented, but in this century - it was more of a success. *Although delving into any property's past, the most well-documented facts are always going to be the sad ones.* His investigation revealed that in the vicinity of the hotel there had been two *mysterious, unexplained deaths* in the past which he found quickly, being more recent.

Not more than ten years ago, a woman's body was found deep in the woods, she had gone missing on the All Hallows' Eve, nonetheless.

A shiver went through Sebastian's body when he made this discovery about this guest's death and the timing of it. Traditionally All-Hallows Eve and the few days following are the beginning of a three-day celebration in many parts of the world, remembering all the souls that have passed on to the afterlife, helping them cross over or just to greet their loved ones.

Is this a coincidence, it being now just upon them?

He immersed himself more deeply in the story. They looked for her for many days even after the celebrations had passed, until they found her.

The surrounding forests were wild in their nature, for somebody to be wandering, it is unwise to get caught up in it. Especially at night and unprepared, in disagreeable weather.

The wilderness here is still intact.

Then Sebastian looked at the other one, even further back in history: the man from 20 years ago. *The man who was found also perished in the nearby woods.*

This happened in the 1950's. Not many records for this one, it remained unexplained. It wasn't even known whether this man had been staying at the hotel as a guest. Nobody from the hotel, *which was just freshly open at the time*, was able to confirm any such thing. *That he was a guest.* Who was he, then? All guest records of the hotel from that time were already lost, so not much to go on. No records to be found nowadays, *how convenient.*

The man was found in a clearing between the trees, already near the dunes that are leading to the beach.

There was a cold draft coming in his direction, he got up to close the door. Warm his hands at the small fireplace for a short while. The laughter of the guest from the main hall, was just now reaching him only as small echo.

He was thinking. So, there is evidence that strange things had happened here before – strange indeed. It remained uncertain to Sebastian whether these two deaths were even connected, and about their connection to the manor house. The circumstances of each death, what really happened, were a mystery. The newspaper put out as a warning not to go wandering out in the woods at night, but nothing more was ever added.

He decided to get back to it. Now feeling a bit warmer. When Sebastian read it again, *he got a different feeling.* It all sounded quite familiar.

And soon... There was one more thing.

One more event.

He spoke with one of his colleagues on the landline. Sebastian and his contact dug a little deeper. They asked him, "Haven't you heard the story? It is well known..."

He hadn't, he answered truthfully.

This was much more dramatic.

In the late 1920s, a young woman had been beaten to death in one of the hotel's rooms, by her older husband. At that time, it was not a hotel, it was a family home.

He was aggressive. Repeating himself.

Anger.

Sebastian was getting strange flashes in front of his eyes.

They were the owners of this house. The builders. And designers.

Suddenly he knew.

She was very beautiful... a party girl, much admired.

The star of society: 'Estrella', they used to call her. Meaning a *star* in Spanish.

That was not her name, of course!

Sebastian read all about them in very old newspaper coverage.

He was overcome by confusion...and shook his head to try to clear a ringing in his ears. He was still in shock, when he tried to remember what had happened to him and Mark the previous night. The way he wasn't able to move his body came *rushing* back to him.

Estrella, a star, a shining star...oh god.

...there was a melody in his head that he could not place, and but at the same time he couldn't forget. He slammed the binder shut exasperated and a cloud of dust came rushing up from it.

He now remembered Mark, sleeping on the sofa, so peacefully.

He began to feel uneasy and his stomach was churning. He had to get out of the library: he almost stumbled out into the main foyer. He braced himself against one of the ornate columns, just to keep himself steady.

This brought enquiring looks from guests walking by. Especially because he could not explain what was wrong with him, when they tried to ask. "Heavy drinking..." they whispered.

He went up the stairs and onto the first-floor landing and found that he felt better. As if some threat that had been hanging over him was gone. He could stand upright again. And think clearly.

He returned to the problem of the unexplained disappearances and deaths in the woods on All Hallows' Eve, at least in his head. The facts he was holding: they were significant, he knew.

It must all mean *something*.

The disappearances in the woods were definitely unexplained. To disappear so deep, inside, as if the forest was swallowing them whole. He was still confused, yet so sure of its importance. *Thick foliage and dark green leaves crumbling beneath his feet, he felt trapped, lost...* He would tell Mark everything, when he saw him again.

But now he must get some rest for a while. Just for a moment, he laid down on his comfortable still made-up bed and closed his eyes. Got to dreaming, a bit...

His life being played out in front of him as in a newspaper. He used to be always more of an outdoors man. Preferring to be on the shore, *gathering the cattle and taking care of the sheep*. Witnessing the colours of the ocean, and roaming under a sky that was constantly changing. From golden hues, to deepest indigo and to breath-taking blue, as it is usually breath-taking here. He never minded when the weather worsened: he simply put his collar up and welcomed the rain, as he made his way back home through the wet fields. They got a lot of this moody weather here in Ireland. And the always-green pastures - which explained its nickname, the Emerald Isle. *This is how he liked it, this is how we would stay.* He was at peace, alone.

But his mother had told him that this lifestyle was not for him – he must try to join the "civilised" world... *Get a civilised job.* To be better off, *and still take good care of his talents, as she called it.* Always being there for him, always taking care of him, if things got difficult.

She wanted him to be better appreciated and welcomed. To build a good reputation. And so, he did. She was just afraid for him, concerned that this job, being outside all the time, may make him even more isolated than he already was. Wanted a proper life for him, so that he could shine.

And so, he had. Listened to his mother... He complied. To gain respect.

"Don't bring these people home with you!" His mother used to say to him.

Because he did. Not literally, but in a way.

He would meet someone, get an understanding of them, even *see into* them – then, like this, they would become a part of him. And the other person – they may not even be aware of it. Or they might. Involuntarily, they became a part of his thoughts, his feelings. And there was no way to put them back.

They were his inner world. His entertainment.

Maybe he would help the person out with something. That was what he did.

And then when it was solved – they would leave him behind. Not needing him anymore. Not looking back. Suddenly, without warning. This only left Sebastian... surprised, *just* surprised.

He never got anything back from them, really.

So, he decided to be always moving. Never returning once to the same place, not if he could help it. This gave him a freedom of sorts. He could do as he liked. Leave. *Or come in.*

He was never expected anywhere.

There suddenly was a smudge of glitter in front of him, a foreign house, different music... this was not his world. Where was it from then? Getting into his dreams. He did not like it here. He wanted to get back. He kept turning over on his bed, trying to wake up.

And in return, he had no expectations. It gave him freedom to listen to his inner call.

He could let it guide him. He could do whatever he liked, whenever he felt like it. He was still doing a job of sorts. Usually being paid for it, he was now working on historical research, with an actual boss and even deadlines. That made him feel nonetheless, *all the same.*

And he just carried the people he had met with him... wherever he went.

But almost never allowed himself to be seen by the outer world.

Not even by friends, not ever. Always on the move.

And all of this led him here tonight.

From the rain into the creaky door of the warm–lit reception. The eyes of the two receptionists staring at him. Eyes open wide. *Feeling dread and excitement at the same time.*

Yes, like this Sebastian would describe his life.

It was all out of the ordinary.

He opened his eyes suddenly, jolted out on the bed. As if in shock, he got used to his surroundings. An old hotel room, in a beautiful house. A lonely complimentary bottle of champagne on the side table waiting to be opened. Quiet all around, just a few piercing birds calling for attention outside. A shard of a dream came back to him, what he must have been dreaming right now... *A girl with a smile, diamonds sparkling, covered in blood. Starlight.* The feeling of emptiness returned to his stomach, and he did his best to shake it off straight away. While navigating himself out of bed into an upright position. Getting his confidence and self-assurance back. After all he was not here for fun, nor for rest. He must get back to Mark, right this moment.

Putting on his shoes he thought about it in more detail. What will he even tell him, where to start? Also, he was feeling hungry, but there was no time for that now. Sebastian decided that he must start by telling Mark what had happened during the night.

If Mark didn't believe him...so, be it!

No, he would, Sebastian was sure.

Perhaps some small memories of Mark's own experiences of the previous strange nights would come back to him. Recollections of events from before Sebastian arrived at the hotel.

Mark was probably not sleepwalking at all. *Wide-awake*, wandering around the hotel, even the grounds, was it so? He may have been even more lucid and active then he himself during last night.

Sebastian would do his best to help Mark to remember. He felt it was important.

But nothing tangible had actually happened last night.

It was getting late. One hour till noon.

Now he had to get going, back to the room Mark was in.

He might already be up.

Eleventh Chapter

Thursday 31th October, Late Morning

Mark

IT WAS THE MORNING. Quite late. Relaxed rays of sunshine were coming through the window, now without the curtains closed.

Mark had woken up quite suddenly. After a few moments getting used to his surroundings, he suddenly felt full of energy. *And realized he had unexpected company.*

He was glad that Sebastian was here. And thankful that he had stayed. Mark went to the bathroom, then made them some coffee, and offered him some toast. He had felt remorse that Sebastian hadn't gotten any sleep. Yet Sebastian didn't mind, the events of last night quite made up for it, *the excitement.* He now remembered everything, *every detail.* He was curious if Mark had remembered anything at all.

Sebastian had looked at his surroundings - it all looked quite cozy for the time-being. Mark made him feel welcome, quite comfortable. *Which was good.* He could be at ease, at least for a while. He finally relaxed.

When he looked at Mark's face, in the morning light, he seemed so innocent and wide-eyed that no one would guess he could not remember events or possibly terrors of nights gone by. Any signs of fear in Mark's eyes from last night were gone.

He was almost excited, out of breath, waiting to hear from Sebastian of the happenings of last night. Mark had such a wonderful aura of needing protection around him. Sebastian was sure that was viewed as attractive, and that other people felt it around him too. And he was yet again pulled in by it.

Mark: "So how was it? Nothing has happened?"

Sebastian was looking for the right words. He took a sip of the coffee offered.

"Was I moonwalking?" he continued, sat a bit closer to him now.

The events now again started to feel to Sebastian like some kind of dream to him, as if far away and elusive.

In such a comfortable, quiet atmosphere, his mind found it difficult to concentrate.

Mark was easy, accessible, friendly and open towards him right away. Maybe it also had happened to other people, around him. That they too had felt the need to protect him. Sebastian thought that the image Mark projected to the outside world was not necessarily a reflection of the kind of person he really was. On the inside his new friend looked that he may be indeed very sharp, decisive and always going after his own interests. In fact not making him a good person in the traditional sense of saying. With all these traits being connected to him - admiration of his peers, his eagerness to please, to get ahead and succeed in what he wants – might all be just a game to him altogether simplifying to him how to take advantage and exploit his peers to get what he wants.

He got him talking more and more. Sebastian was feeling a bit startled, just like he was only watching the scene. Mark was now holding his breath, or maybe breathing very slightly. His eyes were intense and full of expectation.

Sebastian started, no reason to put the suspense off any longer.

She was here. A woman.

Mark looked perplexed. Who?

A ghost.

It was slowly dawning in on him. Sebastian thought he would believe him.

Then something happened. The perplexed look in Mark's eyes changed into something entirely different. *Remembering.*

He was for sure remembering something:

"A beautiful girl..."

Could be anybody.

"A girl with long blonde hair...with curls in them."

Well, that was closer to home, Sebastian gasped.

The new friend still wanted to go steady on Mark.

Where were these memories coming from?

But still Sebastian jumped right into a question –

"You remember something about last night!?"

"Last night? No." Mark was confused. "...You were here, and then nothing ... I must have fallen asleep."

A wild bird flew flapping passionately outside their window, breaking their concentration.

"Not from that night. *But before.*"

A small smile danced on Mark's cheeks, as if a child that finally got his allowance. Figured out what something was.

Still curious about *her*. He continued: "But the days before yesterday: that's when!"

He jumped to his feet, moved around his sofa, thinking aloud.

Sebastian found it difficult to calm himself as well now.

Mark's snow-white complexion, starting with his big dark eyes, ending with a pale face like the snow. His face almost romantic looking, he looks like a prince, but now after recent events his nerves completely shot. A lean body, nimble and fast.

But Sebastian was surprised how easily he also succumbed to his new friend's charm - that he did not expect from himself.

"A woman. Me with her. Outside... We were walking, running.

I felt happy.

Carefree.

Out on the fields..." Mark began gesturing. "Near the sea.

But not quite at it."

He looked through the balcony window in a certain direction, as if he could really see the ocean.

"...never quite near," he said in a whisper, as to himself.

He was slowing down a bit.

Something was taking a hold of him.

Realization.

"I would never go to such a place, on my own... At night. That is not for me."

Her beauty. Her promise of her love – it was so exciting!

Mark looked at Sebastian now, as if expecting him to be happy for him.

Now he continued further.

"Mud on my feet, the wet grass.

Tall trees.

Old ones – the woods?

Wild smell of juniper and pines.

And of the salt on her lips."

His big brown eyes had a tender look to them. So precious.

Just descriptions, he was concentrating, pronunciation clear:

"The sound of the waves, not far away. *Passionate crashes, endlessly, on the shore...* To which we were getting closer to... " Salt in the air and on her lips. "Who was she?" Mark said.

Suddenly lucid. Looking straight at his guest.

As if Sebastian was supposed to hold the answers.

"I myself would never go outside!?

...At night.

Mud on my shoes..." Mark looked quite surprised at himself.

Sebastian could see, he was quiet.

Sebastian was watching his new acquaintance, mesmerized. Even when he didn't understand what he was saying completely, he was taking him with him to these dreamscapes.

Only for Mark: it was his reality.

Pale all over, as if a bit fearful and timid.

Pale as if after a long sickness.

This makes him moody, maybe unsure - and thus closed off.

To Sebastian, Mark looks like a person who is open and friendly, but really lives a very private life inside, without really getting close to anybody.

He doesn't want to share himself with other people, just the things that are on the surface, not those which run deep. He solves everything on his own, rather than showing weakness to anybody.

In his whole self he seems fragile, delicate, as if a strong wind could blow him straight out. Maybe to this he owes the natural ability to bring out the protective streak in people, a need to look after him, just in case.

Then they spoke more, further on.

There was a woman – she took me into the fields, the woods.

What an unbelievable experience, memories like... memories from a different world, as if it wasn't even me.

To the woods in the mud, I wouldn't even go!

He repeated:

But her easiness, her beauty, a promise of love?

The wild smell of purple thistles.

Passionate crashes of the ocean, which they were getting closer to.

The salt all around and on his lips.

The cheeks blushing with crimson. The adornments in her hair. Butterflies made of silk.

The ocean is getting closer again. The dunes of sand.

His legs are moving him closer. But to his surprise, the sand is warming to his skin.

Mark talks to her, about his experiences, his life, adventures, stories from other parts of the world. About himself. About his life.

But he doesn't understand everything about it, this experience. Something about this whole thing is getting away from him. *She is getting away from him.*

To the touch she is so soft, white. Her cooling skin, it always somehow slips away from his fingers. "Let's go, closer to the sea...so we can finally be together, all together...!" she says,

"The water is so lovely now. This time of night."

He just can't no more, can't go further. His shoes are sinking into the soft but deep sand, under his feet it is wet, uncomfortable for him. It just does not feel right.

He wants to go back.

Back to the hotel.

He goes with her... Mark sees the hotel, from a distance.

The house is dark, dark all around.

As if only a few candles were lit in the windows, that was all the light there was.

A sweet quick melody breaks through to them, like the sound of slow jazz.

Not in the air, around him.

He is a bit startled – what is this?

He now walks to the railings of the iron stairs, that lead to the balcony of his room.

The stairs are covered in climbing ivy and the intoxicating smell of wisteria blooms – shouldn't they be here another time of the year, not now? *In the summer?*

"Aren't the flowers beautiful?" She says, satisfied.

As if in a dream land.

"We can do whatever we want to, we have to...." she smiles at him sweetly.

Before the railing steps she says:

"But no! Not there. Don't go there!

There I do not go."

She stops in front of his room. On the balcony.

She knows, he is there in the room, she can feel it: always.

"Let's go somewhere else...

Back again," she insists, pulling him back onto her chest now.

"I know all the hiding places, the shortcuts...everywhere, anywhere but here!

Entrances into the house that I know. Secret passageways, and the hidden entrances.

The doors keep opening up in front of her, that woman he is with.

They are now inside.

In all sorts of bedrooms.

Always in a bedroom that is empty - she knows! Clean and waiting...beautiful and restful. Flowers on linens, blooming on the curtains. Sweet cream, color of peaches, and grass.

Mark sees it all.

And suddenly - here they are together – he and this girl.

He doesn't even remember how.

Did he spend the second night as well with her?

And then he wakes up in the morning.

Mark continues, saying this to Sebastian:

The bedcovers all around him.

He wakes up in the empty bedroom.

Alone. The sun.

For a second time, he was there with her.

In the morning he couldn't remember anything. How did he get there?

Now he has a memory: *It is coming back to him.*

In flashes.

Laughter, the feathers from the covers swaying slowly in the air, *her face.*

More he doesn't remember.

So that's it. A quick smile:

"This is it."

Mark looks in the distance for a while as if lost in his thoughts.

Sebastian is taking *it all in*, he is finding it difficult to shake off the whole atmosphere of the things Mark was telling him right now, it sounded *so beautiful, dream-like... inviting.* How is that possible, Sebastian thought to himself.

He could feel it as well.

How could it have this effect on himself, even just hearing about it? He thought himself more immune than that!

As if he was under a spell.

But all those things…they sounded so horrifying in fact. As if his companion had no control over what was happening to him. He was in a frenzy.

But now - when he looked at Mark - still just staring into the distance quietly - this told a different story. If he was worried a moment ago about himself, that he might be spellbound, he can take one look at the young man and it was clear, his new friend *was spellbound.*

Now almost sadness coming on all over his face.

His eyes black and abandoned.

As if he was not even there. He looked so unlike himself. Like a pale statue…

What is she, this seductress, and what has she been doing to him?

Sebastian got to his feet, with more force than he intended.

Mark said, "So that was her. Have you seen her, or talked to her?"

Traces of tears glistened in his eyes.

"Get something to eat, order something. Get some rest. Gather your strength…" Sebastian replied. "I will tell you all about it when I come back." His thoughts were already on something else. He felt that Mark should be left alone for a while now.

So it wasn't not too much for him to take in.

"I will come back soon, I promise. Stay here."

There was something he needed to find out first.

There was still the library waiting for him, and he had arranged to get a package from town this afternoon, with some information he needed. *He must try to come up with some answers, if that was possible. See if something seems to make sense to him with regards to what is happening here - to what he is feeling and sensing. To see whether it fits.*

Then he could talk about it.

Then hopefully it will make a clearer picture to Sebastian. But he is afraid...it might turn the situation to be even more terrifying than it seemed at first glance.

Mark agreed, and Sebastian left him to his own devices.

"Estrella: what a strange name to have...!" Sebastian said to himself as he left through the hotel room door.

Twelfth Chapter

Thursday 31st October, Noon
Sebastian

SOMETIMES SEBASTIAN'S DREAMS WOULD GIVE HIM ANSWERS. This might be the case again, only he was having no sleep at all, at least not as much as he needed. So, it seemed that dreams wouldn't help this time.

The cold in the library was getting to his bones, so he took a small sip of his tea. The fire was lit on the other side of the room, but it was still too early to have any effect.

He was sitting here alone for some time.

While he was waiting for the fire to warm up the room again, he had a moment to get back to his dreams he had before noon, the parts about himself. So weird and telling at the same time.

As if seeing himself - the minute you had him: he was there and then he was gone.

As though he had never been there, some may say.

Unattainable. Unreachable.

But he liked it that way.

Just out of everyone's reach.

Or memory.

It could be that that was his aim.

He truly was a lone wolf. His clothes being slightly old-fashioned, greyish blue and grass green shades that seemed to reflect in his eyes. That is how he saw himself when he walked into a room: greyish, with sleek fur but a dangerous look in his eyes! His appearance was manly, but still his face was elusive.

He had a courageous, unshakeable look in his eyes and he tended to make an intimidating impression on others. His body was nicely built; you could see he was quite an outdoors man.

Even though he had an almost ethereal quality about him, it was important for him to take care of his body. *To be*

present in his body. What more do we have? He sometimes took it to the limit. He would tackle rain, cold and hills. It was a breeze for him. So, he kept himself in shape.

But his mind: that was another story – he didn't like people venturing there! Trying to work out what was going on inside his head. And he also tried to not hold on to people that much. Just let them go. But that is not an easy quest.

The warm was now getting back to his body. He was suddenly feeling as if the heady smell of orange flowers and honey was gone.

His lips formed a tight line and gave him rather a stern look, but he was still attractive.

Well, but he could put on the charm, when he wanted to. But mostly he kept to himself. He was his own best company.

But perhaps that was about to change.

The other part of his dream slowly came back to him: red lips sipping out of an elegant glass, ankles swirling unhidden, shouts.

He let the newspaper clippings all slip from the envelope, they fell out in front of him on the table. He had received the envelope from the concierge, arriving for him after noon. The old newspaper clippings had been selected because they covered things of interest. They were from old magazines, interviews about the incidents, gossips in a crime journal about the cases connected to the manor house. Speculation, unsolved mysteries, local folklore...

All put together by one of his curious predecessors at some point in the past.

Seeing the old papers and pictures in front of him suddenly made him feel warmer.

The fires of the past.

Those that someone had put out a long time ago... Others that no one ever did.

Thirteenth Chapter

Thursday 31ˢᵗ October, Afternoon
Sebastian

MARK WAS STILL IN HIS ROOM WAITING FOR HIM WHEN SEBASTIAN CAME BACK. He had had a quick lunch. He told Mark everything he had found out since the morning. And then he went on to tell him even more. He started at the beginning, with information about the first owners of the house.

The builders. The wild parties. Her beauty. Prohibited love.

Almost 70 years ago. Well-known enough to have been written about.

A violent act. It was all there. Almost out of a work of fiction. Only difference: it was all true. He told him all about Estrella, the builder's wife, and her story.

Mark was excited, it all interested him very much. Gave sense to the way he was feeling right now, somewhat. *Is that even possible?*

He was amazed.

So grateful to Sebastian that he was here.

"These are all stories, ancient history. I wouldn't have believed it, or put so much effort into researching, if I hadn't seen it here last night. *She was here.*"

Sebastian tried to hide his shiver; Mark didn't notice.

"But you are sure of it - was it not maybe just a dream you had?" Mark put forward. "The girl. The ghost. And you had fallen asleep after all." But the look on the young man's face when putting the questions actually gave out *no doubt* about believing Sebastian's story.

As if Mark knew that already. That it was true.

In two days, I am going to be murdered in this room... This is what she told him?

"But there is all the other stuff, we have enough information - from the other incidents and events, from the "real" world to help you...to understand," said Sebastian.

All Hallows' Eve. That is tonight. When everything had supposedly happened – to Estrella.

Mark just kept on blinking vacantly, as if it was something that did not concern him.

Then when Mark spoke, it went something like this:

"The hotel has a history of murders and sudden disappearances, around this area.

Since it was built. Of course it is not something they will tell you when you come to stay. There is of course the infamous demise of its owner's wife.

So he beat her to death right here in this room?"

"I don't know where. It...maybe.

She was supposed to be leaving with her lover... Charlie.

That is what she called you right here..."

Sebastian pointed to the sofa, where she held Mark's sleeping face in her arms.

"And you let her? A ghost..."

"There was nothing I could do. It was as if I was glued in one place. I couldn't move until it was all over."

Which was true, yet Sebastian did feel a small jolt of shame when he told him that. How was *that* protecting him?

"She was being..."

And it was all so beautiful.

"She was being tender with you, so kind." Sebastian continued.

Mark just looked puzzled, he was frowning as he was thinking.

"I am sorry I don't remember that." he said suddenly. <u>So quietly.</u>

<u>As if in pain.</u>

"How could I sleep through such a thing..."

Now it dawned on Sebastian: "It was because I was here. She didn't wake you. You didn't go with her, anywhere. Like you had the previous nights. She drew back after a while.

I was in her way... So I did protect you, in a way."

Mark sighed and relief flooded his face.

"Then everything is okay. It will be all right.

Just as long as you stay here with me."

Mark was on his feet, walking around.

Then suddenly he sat down, very close to Sebastian. He was like a puppy on adrenaline.

"Yeah," Sebastian said uncertainly, "...but I should probably tell you the rest of what I have found out about the house. There is more you should know about the history of murder over this last century. There is more since whatever happened to Estrella, and not that long ago. *Disappearances.*"

"Yeah? But who did it?"

"They never found out."

Sebastian told it like this:

"Since the house was converted in the late 40s into a hotel for travellers, two of its guests have mysteriously vanished. Later they were found dead under unknown, and apparently unnatural circumstances, in the woods. The incidents had happened many years apart, so it never struck people to connect them together and nor did it create much gossip about this place. And nobody really remembers much about it now.

But the police information is still available.

The first report was from the 1950s. One morning a man was found, impaled on a sharp tree stump, deep in the woods beyond the hotel. It all looked like an accident, that he had fallen onto it while taking a stroll. But when the police inquiries got to it, it didn't seem natural at all, the force with which he had met his fate was too strong.

The second incident was closer to our current time. A woman, in the 1980's: she came here on her birthday party, as well."

Mark blinked again.

"She was staying in this room, your room. Her name was "Charlene", but all the people who knew her just called her "Charlie"! After dusk fell, very late at night, as witnesses testified, they would hear a voice from the garden,

underneath the window – someone calling her name. Calling out for her: "Charlie! Charlie!"

Some admirer they supposed, they laughed. She was from around these parts, someone from her past most probably? Or maybe a lady lover! Because it sounded to them almost like a woman's voice...some had said. That was one of the theories... The witnesses couldn't recognize, came to an agreement, what kind of voice they really had heard. Was it a man's, or a woman's? Perplexing.

An ordinary woman the lady guest had been, one known as quiet. "Charlene was stunned. She didn't know what kind of business this was." This went on for two nights. A voice outside calling for her. After that, when they couldn't find her - they thought she had left the evening shindig early - with her mystery lover. Not much mystery there. But then, nobody could find her.

After five days a bird watcher found her body, again deep in these woods. In a place where nobody usually ever goes, that deep...lying peacefully in a clearing, dead from exposure to the elements.

There was a shockwave in her closest circle and the local community. A mystery. What had happened to Charlene? Why she did go out, out there to the woods?

Was she alone or not?

Nobody ever came forward, with any information.

This had happened much closer to the seashore, then the previous man. And it was quickly added as another one of the unexplained deaths surrounding the hotel and its woods."

They were quiet for a long time.

"Oh, golly…" Mark had said, still imaging the facts in his head.

It was nearing 6 o'clock.

"We must get ready for the party. The big celebration."

"What?" Sebastian had asked.

It was almost evening, again.

He was always up for a good party…the evening tux in the twenties style he borrowed for the occasion lay ready. "Are you sure…" Sebastian proposed.

"Yes, of course. Just if you stay with me tonight, for sure…everything will be all right".

The All Hallows' Eve party was just starting. Or as it is, you could say 31st October…but that is just the way it is celebrated on the day out here.

Sebastian was thinking that in the next few nights there would be huge bonfires lit here, on and around the shore. The lights usually glistening and amplifying its reflection on the water as a tradition, leading the souls of the dead to find their way home, or out of purgatory.

The biggest night for the birthday girl it seems: her celebration. *Her actual birthday.*

It was a costume party, but they were not celebrating Halloween - as Mark has told him - they are celebrating **her**. They are to be in costume - an elegant twenties theme, as the whole stay, but it is not supposed to be scary. She wanted it like this her whole life… Well not everybody is "lucky" to be born on this day, Mark explained to him.

Then it kind of takes all the attention away from her. *And she wants that attention.*

The sun is setting quickly outside.

"We have to be there." Mark said to him as getting ready, in a low husky voice.

He was preparing in the bathroom. Combing his hair.

Sebastian is ready, got changed in the meantime, now sitting on the edge of the bed.

Not enough time to go back to his room, before dinner starts.

Only there is one thing Mark asks. He turns around facing him, door slightly ajar now:

"Do you think the place is haunted? "

"Every place is haunted," Sebastian answers.

"Depends on its history…and what has happened in such a place. Did the souls leave as they wanted, in peace? Are there parts of the original structure still intact? Or the surroundings."

Sebastian isn't sure if Mark can even hear him, but he continues.

"A haunting brings a strange quality to a place. A fingerprint," Sebastian says, as if trying to explain it to his companion. "Putting the whole place as if into a haze… that is if it has energy enough. And that is usually to be had at night. You know why?

Because that is when it is the most peaceful, when the energies are left undisturbed, with enough veil of the dark to gather. People, households…usually asleep. Forest as well, the animals." *But not the sea...that is alive always. Sebastian hears, as if inside his head.*

He continued, undisturbed: "The spirits have a special ability around them - it is difficult to explain. They are not actually placed in the future, present nor the past. They just exist somewhere...in time. Usually being tied to a place, more than to anything else.

And then they can in our eyes move backward or forward in it.

It is just the same for them. And for a person that is with them...

You see time doesn't exist in the classical linear way we imagine it. There is still much we have to learn about, to understand it fully. *The present and the past, the future... there are all happening at the same time."*

Sebastian lets out a long breath, as if relieved. *That's his theory anyhow.*

"Well...all right. I will try to not think about it right now...!" Mark replies from the open doors of the bathroom, even amidst his movements, surprisingly engaged in what he was saying, "But I will later on, I promise. I will give it some thought..."

Sebastian gives a faint laugh, as if what Mark is saying at that moment is actually funny.

But presently Sebastian underestimates how much Mark may be already under the spell. Fully, as well, and already too deeply. That he can't do much about it.

Underestimating how much Mark may remember about their own conversation, they had just now and this afternoon.

With the sun now completely set, Sebastian looks out through the window and can see and hear crows slowly circling on the ground. They are after some prey, he is caught wondering - or is it just because, it is *today?*

Mark looks out as well. He doesn't like this time of year. Walking down the streets by yourself, as if a strange fog is in your eyes and suddenly you are not alone, on an empty street.

You turn around while hearing the lonely clicking of one carriage horse, then it is gone and there is no-one. A black cat crossing a street.

Leaves falling, then crumpling on the ground. A wind swaying ferociously, the northern kind, getting under your skin. But that is not today. That is yet to come.

The darkness soon to be all around announcing the night, makes Sebastian wonder how much Mark will forget. *It is gone six o'clock now after all.*

On a more happy note, because Sebastian was just put in a good mood: why not distract themselves for a bit with a *good party and food*, after the day and long night they had had?

But as he recalled - not all parties in this house have a happy ending.

Fourteenth Chapter

Ratmulen House, 1927

HE WAS A BANKER, A RICH ONE PER SE, HIS FAMILY BUILT THE MANOR MANY GENERATIONS AGO AND LIVED THERE AND ELSEWHERE EVER SINCE. *His immediate family added to this classical manor in the 1880's and completely doubled the house in size.*

From then on, it was used only as a vacation house. Then in the 1920's he personally continued the work on the house, building new wings which came as a magnificent gift to his bride to be... So she could sit back and soak up the sun by the new large French windows on the more advantageous southern side of the house, when there was the rare period of glorious sunshine. Three bay windows were added as part of the new wing, and the surrounding grounds were extensively planted as a garden, with tropical plants, practical vegetables, lots of roses and a greenhouse. Then the house, gardens and countryside around the house really shone - as bright as ever, as did she.

He met her in Paris, on one of his many business trips, a flapper girl from America. She knew how to enjoy life. He brought her home to Ireland as a blushing bride, straight to his summer country house. Although she was in fact not blushing at all... just the opposite being a young woman of experience, who was looking for joy and pleasure in her life.

Her own glow was so radiating and infamous, in Paris they got used to call her just: "Estrella". And that is what she went by, only that.

The newly married couple had invited many of their international friends to spend a few months with them at a time at the manor house...and they brought along with them a style unheard of in the local area until now. But all happening in the privacy of the walls of the house, these intimate gatherings by the sea.

They were one of the few houses that had a radio installed, always keeping up with the ever-changing times. Or so they tried.

Such a sweet innocent kitten - she was, Estrella, the lady of the house - even in the eyes of the servants.

She enjoyed the house so much - going to sleep in a bedroom in one wing of the house and waking up in another. The staff took turns to look for their mistress in the morning. To bring her hot chocolate, breakfast - to bed. It turned out to be this little game of theirs.

Some say kiddingly that she wasn't always alone...in all these bedrooms. But always alone in the morning – just waiting for her husband, who adored her, and enjoyed her antics. Having a few vices himself, not being a young man! At least in the beginning.

She was liked, she was fun to be around. Never made much of a fuss about anything, was satisfied with almost anything at all, at the same time having such wonderful ideas and inspiration. Creative visions for decorations around the house, meals for guests, purchases to invest in, *fun events to plan – all very new. Jazz music playing out into the night at all hours nonetheless. Her fashion sense and sensibility being impeccable, her material and feather adorning her head always being so smooth and inviting to touch. Leaving a distinct trail of perfume Toujours Moi, being definitely the thing now in Paris, in French fittingly* "Always Me", *which she loved.*

She was very invested in her husband even though he was much older than her.

His sweet innocent kitten.

But the cracks were beginning to show.

*She didn't expect to be closed up all the time in an - eventually - stuffy atmosphere. After the marriage, he forbade her to travel. Not on her own. And **he** couldn't, not any more.*

That came soon with his position, that had changed, as he took on an even larger role in his company. After the death of his brother.

She took it with a brave face.

And then one thing she didn't plan on happened.

She fell in love. Not with her husband.

She didn't want to be locked away.

She wanted to live life to its fullest still - enjoy herself (without restrictions).

The one thing she had not planned for had to happen.

He was around the manor for about two months, stayed there upon invitation of his boss, her husband: and in all that time he and the young lady of the manor hadn't spoken once.

Which was very odd, for Estrella...being her, with her warm, all welcoming character. And the hostess of the house, let's not forget. This was very unusual behaviour for her.

People and surrounding acquaintances embraced her, not the other way around.

They wanted to <u>be</u> in her company.

Doing some work in the vicinity, for her husband. He was an engineer, a scientist of sorts, working during the day... in a way. His nights were free. His smooth brown velvety hair, eyes that shone like daylight. He was so beautiful. Her prince - just for her.

After just once catching <u>each other's eyes,</u> their passion grew endlessly over time.

Never speaking a word to each other though.

Being near to the end of his stay...he was supposed to be leaving.

They have yet to speak to each other still, but it was as if they didn't need it. As if this was enough for them. All was transmitted internally.

She took him into her room – her own r e a l bedroom this once.

They were quiet, they didn't speak. <u>They kissed</u>. He held his hands around her waist, tenderly.

They stopped. She laid her head on the pillow of the bed, laying her legs smoothly on him sitting, on his lap, so he could feel her warmth.

Dressed in silk-white reflecting stockings, her skirt going slightly upward while she lay down. They didn't go any further. As if there was nowhere to.

What they were feeling in that moment, just being near each other, was too much for them.

It only made her sad. Charlie said to her: "Run away with me".

Her crystal earrings shaped as bright stars jangled as she moved.

All very innocent one would say. But was it?

Fifteenth Chapter

Thursday 31st October, Dinner
The Birthday Party: Sebastian

She was standing in the doorway.

The festivities were in full swing.

The girls were laughing, running around in their dresses, *sparkly things, moist lips.*

Suddenly no-one could feel the upcoming cold from outside of the fall evening – everyone was so warm. *It was All Hallows' Eve.*

She stood in the doorway, *as if she was invited.* Her dress – spot on.

Magnificence itself. For a period costume party, set in the 20's, she fitted right in.

Of course, she did.

She moved inside with a velvety-soft step, the tip of her slippers touching the floor delicately.

A breeze of the sea air came with her, faint cries of the seagulls, for a split second.

The doors were being kept open, holding themselves ajar with a whirlpool of air.

Two bellboys had to push them shut, and lock them, just to keep them from opening again.

She was standing inside, finally.

She glided in serenely, but with feet firmly on the wood floor. She nodded and said something in the sense: *"Hello, thank you for having me…"*

Sebastian just stared in disbelief. But he was not surprised. She had grown stronger. Thanks to him and his energy, which he was putting into the situation: he was afraid to admit. She smiled at him sweetly. *Estrella.*

She could now enter the house. In full human form, and with no-one the wiser.

She caused quite a commotion around herself. All were in awe of her. *"What a perfect dress!"*

As if they knew her. *That is how they acted.* As if they were all already under her spell.

Spellbound, because nobody inside, once they laid eyes on her same as Sebastian – never considered that they didn't know who she was. *"This is amazing. She is so beautiful."* *They had gushed on.* She had received the compliments *gracefully. Eyes sparkling like stars indeed.*

The admiring stares of men. Her dress was peach, with delicate bronze rhinestones shining. *Perfect down to every detail.* The smooth silk of the gloves. The out-worldly star pin in her hair. Pearl earrings dangling, her nails a bright red.

Such an elegant shoe - with straps and a small kitten heel, with an embroidered dark see-through veil over her hair and discretely covering her arms and décolletage of such *plush* skin *shining* underneath it.

But she was still *too white* in Sebastian's eyes. Had that ethereal glow about her.

Nobody seemed to notice.

And nobody seemed to care.

The admiration of men aimed in her direction was welcomed in her coquettish eyes. Even Sebastian couldn't help but to just keep on looking at her. She looked like a woman who knew what she was doing. *Seated at the table now.*

Her alabaster skin, beautiful green eyes, with specks of gold.

Light hair catching the light of the candles on the table and hung from the ceiling, giving off a soft strawberry sheen.

The party was gleaming. *Lots of lights everywhere.* White party balloons hung from the ceiling above the table. There was a small dancefloor and a smartly dressed band. Centerpieces of *pink gladiolas*. A small pyramid of golden champagne in coupe style glasses, stacked one on top of the another, was the final theme touch.

Candlesticks on the table shone too brightly when you wanted to look at your neighbour opposite, deep into their eyes.

Jellied appetizers were a treat back in the day, all kinds of fruits made in jelly. Next to them lay pineapples cut through the middle, lemon cupcakes, pimiento salad... all inviting to take a delicious bite right away. And to talk and gush about them with their friends afterwards.

That was the party tonight.

Highball in hand, you couldn't look away. *Gifts for the birthday girl, ribbons flooding the table, with glitter falling off them down to the floor.*

Amongst everything, everybody still staring at *her.* Women admiringly at her dress: *how detailed*! They happily welcomed her into their society.

Even Sebastian had to stare at her all the time, while the food was being served... He was unhappy – disgusted and surprised by his own reaction.

In shock, he worried at the same time: Where will all this lead? And what part in it will <u>he</u> be playing? And where is *Ch...*Mark?

And who is...*Charlie, anyway*?

Sebastian was thinking this to himself, not letting his mind go in any other direction.

But on the other hand, **why not dance with a ghost?!**

He asks her to the dance floor.

Small lights flickering. Other couples having fun. Hems of the skirts twirling.

She says "yes".

The music.

What starts as a happy tune now turns slower.

He holds her closer to himself, as almost as if he could feel her - but not entirely... He squeezes more tightly: he *almost* feels her warmth.

Making out with a ghost...why not?

She is fragile and smooth. He can feel from her that she is an experienced dancer, to do this type of jazz tune, anyway. But it still seems that her every move is very precise, a slow and calculated movement, never too abrupt. *She is concentrating on her every step very deeply. It is taking her effort.* Yet to a distant eye her movements are lovely and uninterrupted.

With of course a good dancing partner at her side, she pulls it off...

Leading herself, where she wants to go.

Carefully, in rhythm, smoothly, along with the music, which is changing now into a wild beat again. Never changing her movements, as if she couldn't do it any other way. So meticulously. *Sebastian* can feel her holding her breath. At the end now he lifts his hand and slowly moves her body around into a pirouette. Leads the girl into a spin, all the way around... as the music is drifting away.

His dance partner manages, even though the tension is palpable all around them, with elegance and playfulness. The song is ending. She offers him a small kittenish smile, as if to say: *See what I can do? When I want to?* But then the music continues on again.

"Leave him alone. He doesn't want you."

"*Oh, yes he does. He already loves me entirely, almost.*"

A dazzling echo around them, as if a memory.

The music is now a gentle quiet sway. He holds her closer again, but not entirely this time, so they can talk better. They continue with their dance.

"It's not like that. He doesn't even know about you... remember you, when he is lucid. "

She sees into his misdirection:

"*But I...need, want, his help. It is only 2 days, then he will kill me.*"

"You are already dead. That won't happen." Sebastian is confronting her.

She continues to sway on, her voice a sweet whisper to the music, never once letting go in her decisiveness: "*I need his help...*"

"He doesn't think about you, and he doesn't want you. At all."

She smiles at this, her lips twisting into a smirk.

"*That is a lie. He will be mine.*

I know that, I can feel it!"

And you will more likely help with this, then the other way around!

She smiles at him coquettishly. She laughs a small laugh. Dancing she is swaying her hips agreeably... Slowly they are leaving the dance floor.

Alabaster skin, full rich bosoms hidden. The big soft light above their heads flickers. As if it was under some strange strain, continuously.

Sebastian takes her off the dance floor, out of the main hall...just to get out of there for a while. They are holding on to each other, their conversation still ongoing...entering the open, deserted main hallway.

Mark was fine all evening, behaving normally. As if there was nothing special he was paying attention to, nothing out of the ordinary. *As if there is nothing wrong going on.*

He has been like that all evening. Everything they have discussed seems to drift away from his mind. The young man is sitting between two cheerful girls - they being in the same good mood as he is. They entertain him, take care of him during dinner…they play, flirt easily, *without a care in the world for all of them.*

Sebastian is sitting at the head of the table, Mark is attentive to him, pleasant, nothing more.

Not even a casual glance in his direction.

Later they go out to the hallway, Sebastian and his unusual dance partner. *After their dance.*

But the hallway is not abandoned after all.

Mark is kissing passionately with a dark-haired girl, leaning against one of the columns near the stairs. He is already in his element. Quite easy for the others to see… The woman leans and pushes him harder into the column; she is the active one now.

She fawns over him, now placing her back against the wall; kissing him, her arms around his neck. Then Mark senses them behind them, approaching arm in arm.

He turns around.

They both see him, nothing very different about him, staring slightly surprised. *Sebastian and his lady guest*, they were just talking…and this had caught then off-guard, in the middle of a sentence. Talking about *him in fact.*

Their lively discussion suddenly comes to a halt. Their playful argument from the dancefloor now turns into something different.

Sebastian blurts out to her, without thinking: "See, this is what I mean."

About Mark. He doesn't care about you.

Just to prove himself right.

Mark is slowly turning his eyes to them, lets himself be interrupted in the moment. He is looking at them, in this way: *what is the problem?* A bit surprised at the *commotion caused.* He sees Sebastian, that is for sure. At closer inspection he is looking directly at both, he sees both of them for sure.

Even her. But to the woman with Sebastian…he has no reaction to her.

None at all.

He doesn't recognize her.

Now lazily unfazed Margaret turns to face them as well, her black eyes slightly annoyed yet still so smug. *Especially when she sees the other girl.*

They wriggle out of each other's arms a bit.

And then suddenly she is gone. Estrella is gone.

A whirlpool of wind lifts up, catching the light and specks of dust in the air.

Kissing another!

The doors are suddenly open, without anybody seeing how it happened, almost hanging out of their hinges.

Just a cold draught.

Sebastian is standing there all alone.

Sebastian turns back to them and on semi-automatic he asks: "*...where is she?*"

But already he knows she is gone. "Who?" Mark asks vacantly...

"...she is gone." Just a quizzical look is left in Mark's eyes.

As if Mark knew something was happening, he could just not place what.

He didn't remember her.

He didn't recognize her. Or even see her for that matter!

Sebastian is anxious and angry.

The other man is sensing his mood but doesn't know what to say. Margaret leaves.

"What are you doing?" Sebastian steps a bit closer to Mark, so that their conversation is kept private. Again, pressing Mark against the wall, he does get a whiff of his aftershave, *what a Casanova his new friend is.*

That he even notices the scent is bothering him.

Even himself, falling underneath his boyish charm? Is it so easy?

"What do you mean? That girl? That was nothing! I *don't understand* what the problem is anyway..." Mark pushes him away, off of him, readjusting his collar and evening wear.

They are both dressed to the nines...in tuxedos, it is a formal evening after all!

And Mark especially wears it well, he is a natural.

With a sheepish look on his face, that he wasn't doing anything wrong by the way, Mark proclaims: "...so what? I was kissing a girl. What's it to you?" he says slightly annoyed.

Sebastian, mirroring his mood, wanting to knock some sense into his companion, reacts:

"There is real danger in this house. A few people have died already..."

"And what's it got to do with me?!"

"If you want my help... So you don't want my help?" Sebastian continues and goes back into the past for his argument: "The woman who disappeared, Charlene, she was staying in *your hotel room*, I have confirmation now. I dug that much up, through the hotel records. "

He pauses for a while: "Not that they are being very cooperative."

Mark calms down a bit.

His hands, resting on his thighs, are shaking pretty heavily now. As if he was under great duress.

He straightens up, and navigates Sebastian with a gesture towards the staircase, *to get out of the way a bit.*

"Of course I want your help," he says with humbleness.

"Listen, it means the world to me that you are here trying to help, Sebastian."

Sebastian sighs, relaxing. It feels like he got through to him - but how can he be sure? And how can Sebastian protect him? *Protect him from...from what?*

"You must keep safe. Be careful. *Go to your room.*" he says straightforwardly.

It seems right now Mark doesn't mind being ordered around.

"Get some sleep," Sebastian says more tenderly.

Mark was suddenly…as if waking up. As if remembering what was this really about.

"…*close your windows, we will see.*"

It was nearing 9 pm. Was this the time again? *It this when* he wakes up from his amnesia? That doesn't make sense to Sebastian. Or…*the girl* was gone. Disappeared. She is definitely gone for the evening, Sebastian can feel it. So can Mark, he can see it in his eyes. *A tension is gone.*

The girl is no longer with them. Is she the one doing this to him, to Mark? *Enchanting his mind and memory…in a way that suits her. In a way she needs it to be…* Sebastian was thinking. Suddenly Mark in front of him, starts remembering the whole situation. *As if the dark haired man was now waking from a deep sleep. An amnesia.*

From a waking dream. An enchantment, or bewitchment.

Sebastian felt he had been talking to two different Marks at the same time, at this point.

But it was a bit like that.

"It is fine. I will." he whispers.

Mark is one step further up the stairs than Sebastian, retreating from the situation.

"I think she has left. She left me alone yesterday. The ghost.

Whatever she was, it is finished…"

"But she was just here…"

Sebastian says calmly. Patiently. "At the party."

Mark replies: "The woman that was with you? I didn't recognize her." *Mark takes one step back to him, suddenly in no hurry, shocked.* "What, she was here?"

Sebastian now nods in agreement.

"…The girl with you. I have never seen her before…"

Mark is startled.

"You didn't even notice *her at dinner*…"

Mark: "No…"

"She was seated just next to Jamie, near to me…"

"Her? I never even looked in that direction. *As if something was keeping me from looking her way.* As if she was just out of my focus, out of my reach… I haven't even seen Jamie, I haven't seen her all evening," Mark adds.

A saddened, lonely look passes across Mark's face. *Charlie.* He is looking into the distance, from the top step of the stairs towards the entry door, now firmly shut. He is lost.

"I have missed her." Now a look of remorse was on his face.

Sebastian was quite perplexed and worried about his reaction. That is why he was like that the whole dinner. Sebastian was wondering if Mark isn't remembering anything they talked about together previously at all. As if he was…under a spell.

Was this what it was like being bewitched?

117

As if he hadn't seen her at all.

As if there was something shifting his perception, a filtering of it.

So she can move around in the world unhindered, if she wants to.

Directing his attention away from her, so that she goes around unnoticed, at least to Mark.

Or just maybe…. Mark just didn't want to see her…was not yet prepared for it, in these real-life circumstances. And the effect only amplified his feelings…feeding off it.

*So he knew she was there, yet he didn't want to know...
his memory had shifted, and any inconsistencies throughout
the night forgotten.*

*Rendering her thus unnoticeable, just a trick of the
memory for Mark.*

As if by realizing this, his companion was remembering.
Remembering her.

Estrella. Missing her?

It was affecting Sebastian too. Just in another way. He
couldn't actually take his eyes off of her: everything else
was just a blur to him...even Mark. As if this evening she
was here because of Sebastian, not Mark...but why? Were
these her spells, being used on him now? *Caught in her
web as well...*

Just when he, Sebastian, was about to speak: "I can..."

Mark interrupts his words forcefully:

"It is fine. I am going to my room. I will be alone.

He looks straight at him, large eyes, coldly.

"It will be ok. I will shut the windows and the balcony
doors.

Good night."

His worried companion wants to say: "I will join you,
as we agreed..." but something stops Sebastian.

A few quick steps and he leaves Sebastian at the top of
the stairs, going back to his room. Alone.

Leaving Sebastian standing on the staircase, without a
word.

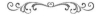

Sebastian loosens up and relaxes a bit finally after a long day, going back to his own room, the smaller one on the ground floor. He had known his new friend just a little over 24 hours, but still it *kinda* of hurt. To be sent away like this.

The garden beyond the small patio door was quiet and dark. They will go over it again together tomorrow, he and Mark. Maybe the other man was right: it was nothing. And it was over. Mark was being so sure when they talked… that it might be all over.

But it may be that he is being naïve.

Or maybe…he is hoping it will all go another way?!

Sebastian feels the need to protect him, even from himself.

Sixteenth Chapter

Friday 1ˢᵗ November, Very Early Morning
All Saints' Day
Mark

THE NEXT DAY MARK WAKES UP IN THE CELLAR, STANDING UP. He doesn't know how he got there.

He doesn't know the place; it is just concrete and pipes. Flooded, with water leaking in. His shoes and the ends of his pants up above the ankle are soaked in water. *The water is slowly dripping in, soaking the floor.* From outside.

It appears to have been raining. *A storm.*

It is quite dark; he has no idea what time of the day it is.

He cannot open the doors to get out.

They are stuck.

It is murky all round him, almost no windows: just little ones up top.

Then the doors give and he gets out. He is in one of the service corridors, leading to the main hotel room hallways, on the ground floor. He steps on the carpet, water dripping from him to the ground. *With every step, splashing.*

He finds his way to the first floor hotel corridor, back at the staircase. All the corridors are deserted and empty. Into his room. He hides. He looks out and it is very early morning outside.

121

He starts to believe *him, Sebastian,* now even more.

He doesn't know where he has been.

What he did all night.

Was he with her again?

His heart is racing. Why doesn't he remember it?

Such terror now he feels…but as if he was waking from a sweet dream. *This is what he feels. What it feels like to him.*

Was she really that woman he saw yesterday at the dinner?

He still can't remember her in detail or place her. Standing there with Sebastian underneath the stairs, staring at him. But he remembers that scene: seeing her with him.

He just can't seem to reach her, find her in his mind - now in a full conscious aware state.

Like a dream he forgot. Mark just doesn't remember.

She is just out of my focus, out of my reach.

She is just beyond his horizon.

His tuxedo from last night is still on.

He feels cold.

Something is not right indeed.

Nobody sees him.

Seventeenth Chapter

Friday 1ˢᵗ November, late Afternoon
Sebastian

LATER THE DAY AFTER THE BIG PARTY SEBASTIAN IS GOING OVER *AGAIN* ALL OF THE DOCUMENTS HE HAS RECEIVED, EVEN THE ONES HE HAD MISSED. That were gathered from the libraries and the research of local historians. As he reads more, he finds information about the deaths in the area of the house, drawn out in much more detail. The further back into the decades he goes, something about this place always pops out. Something off about this place, certainly not ordinary.

People have said the victims have fallen victim to the ghouls of the forest.

Fairies.

These are common in these places. Or meaning maybe, that these kinds of stories are common in these places. But who knows? Maybe it is something so outlandish?

The two incidents never connected; they were too far apart in years from one another to get linked. But, reading now through the newspapers, and even a modern police transcript he got his hands on yesterday – he asked himself: in what way were these people similar?

He goes through it again in his head.

What happened to them, and was it for the same reason? The woman in the 80's, she was a guest at the hotel. Found dead in the clearing in the woods.

The man in the 50's found embedded on the old piece of wood...nobody couldn't find out who he was. A traveler. Not from these parts. That suddenly flashes before his eyes. Was he staying at the hotel also, and were they just afraid to admit it?

Were these two connected? What did they share, have in common? Were they experiencing the same things, just moments before their end, and is that even possible? Was there an identical reason for their demise?

Then he continues on to the old book and photo albums he just found lying in the dust on the bookshelves of the manor's library. Where he is now seated.

Such a coincidence: A history of the place and of the building.

And then of course when he opens it up there is the most talked about <u>owner of the house.</u> The young woman, who has been beaten to death in the grounds, not so long after all the building works were finished. Who was that girl, the flapper girl, and what was she like? When she was alive... *A fate she had met in the house.* Is she tied just to the house?

So, the beauty from the balcony, from the dancefloor yesterday, is that her?

And who knows how many people could have fallen into her trap...

If it *is a trap* she is setting. At all.

He goes over it and through it more times in his head and gets a much clearer picture.

But the picture he does put together is *quite disturbing, to say at least.*

While he is thinking about it…a loose picture, a professional black-and-white photograph falls out of a dusty book.

Onto his knees.

It is her – Estrella.

Her eyes staring back into his.

Peaceful, full of life.

Carefree.

It is *she*, he can be sure now. No one can doubt him. The sun was still up. But the day was going by quickly, it was already the afternoon.

Mark did not look him up.

Sebastian decided to give him some space.

After the argument they had yesterday evening, it seemed like the right thing to do.

He is still here only on invite…his invite.

Now he can tell him and be sure.

Soon after, in the afternoon after the big party, Mark finally comes to him.

He is different, humble, sweet on him.

"Please, don't be mad with me about how I acted last night! Please."

Difficult to resist.

He is calm, but in a good mood, attentive to him.

They go on talking. Even though they have known each other such a short time, it just feels so natural and there is an easy flow. Sebastian is relaxed and Mark is friendly to him, as if he was his good old friend, without any sign of pretending.

They grew close quite quickly. Mark has told him things he hasn't shared with anyone in the last hours from the days gone by.

He behaved openly and acceptably to his self-proclaimed powers, to the reason why he was here. How he felt he was called here, to him.

In a way this is what Sebastian was looking for: an easy connection, somebody he can talk to about his feelings, and not need to lie.

But sometimes these things just happen.

Marks is next to him, with his hands on Sebastian's necktie: "Where are you going?" He drives his hands slowly through the tie until he lets go at the very bottom with his fingers.

Sebastian is not going anywhere, he just presumed that people do dress up for this sort of occasion and that is why he is wearing a suit.

He gets up from the sofa, they are in his own room now, and he walks around it. The ventilator on the window to the garden is slightly open and he closes it. "I must tell you more about what I have discovered about the deaths and disappearances in the area."

"You mean like who *she* is? You know for sure now?

I mean…what may be happening to people when they meet her? "

Sebastian smiles sadly. "Not happy stories to tell."

Mark is not worried about it at all and what it all means, and continues to say: "…maybe it has no connection, none whatsoever to what is happening here now, to me… But maybe it does."

He stands up, melodramatically and proclaims rather suddenly:

"She just wants help…

…he is planning to… he's about to kill her…."

Sebastian is startled - "Who? How do you know that, Mark?"

The mood changes a bit.

"Were you with her again last night?"

Mark is unsettled, exhausted. He doesn't know, again.

Sebastian tells him about the photograph he has found.

He says to the young man next to him: "Stay here. Rather with me."

Mark says: "But I'm not here just for fun, I have work to do…."

"Either way." Sebastian continues, stubbornly, taking hold of the situation. "Don't go out. I beg you." It was getting dark outside.

But tomorrow, we should leave and drive away. That is his final advice to him.

Sebastian is *thinking* that Mark's stay here is not just for entertainment. What does he mean by that? "Why stay here? I don't see any reason for it.

"For all I know, I will stay." Marks eyes shift a little as he explains:

"Let her do what she wants…" His words drift out a little. Giving this whole scene a bit of a different light.

"I don't feel in peril. *Threatened.*"

"How can you talk like that, after all you have heard?

"You're not my boss, you don't get to tell me what to do!"

Mark is getting angrier.

A light that Sebastian sees in his eyes, he feels shaken by.

He wants to see her.

Is that it?

He is under her influence so completely? A complete fool. He tells him that.

Mark goes on being spellbound, a foreign dark look in his eyes.

Not knowing what the fuss is about, he smirks: "I'm not afraid of the wood, and the night, and the sea. The sea I'm not afraid of."

He is so smug.

Has he not heard anything I have said, about this place? The danger.

Sebastian is taken aback, breathless. How can he change anything?

Is this even his place here.

Seeing him, watching Mark so helpless, yet happy, brings out tenderness in his heart. How can he want to take that away from him?

Why are his moods changing so rapidly? Sebastian feels he has no control over him.

No honest way to reach him.

Mark walks around helplessly, pleading - he tries to explain to him.

Yet his eyes are shining, alight from within, in a way he hasn't seen him before.

Sebastian was asking the question what the ghost wants from Mark, the disappeared hotel guests, all on All Hallows' Eve...it had never occurred to him to ask about what Mark could possibly want or need from <u>her</u>?

Mark is laughing with mirth, excitement... *Being able to share it with his friend.*

"It is like *nothing...*" he lays stress on that word, "...I've seen before in my life. *It is the excitement I have been missing.* Even though I don't remember it, I feel so alive these last few days, more than I ever have before."

He wants Sebastian to see, agree with him.

Such a feeling of relief is now coming over Mark, when he is remembering. *He is so calm.*

At times Sebastian cannot understand what Mark is saying: some things he gets perfectly, are sane... And the others feel like *they are from a completely different world.*

His companion continues so self-assuredly:

"Of all the romances I have had, she is different from them. *She is like dynamite.*"

Sebastian cannot recognize him at all.

Yet he feels sorry for him, the longing - he envies him that.

The love that she had put into him.

Talking as if he was figuring out something right now "…only she can complete me."

Be his other half?!

"The fear, that I feel, it is of course just an obvious part of it," Mark explains, as if there is nothing more to discuss.

There are hot streaks running through the parting of his hair. He stands still.

Now all of the room has grown very warm. As if they had been drinking. But they haven't even had a sip of the unopened whiskey standing on the nightstand.

Sebastian goes again to open the window. A call comes from outside, of a guest, a call for dinner presumably. *It is that time of day again.*

It has all gone by so quickly.

It is pitch black outside, but now there are stars coming out right through the clouds.

Sebastian: "Are you so much under her spell that you are willing to sacrifice yourself, for her, as well? "

Mark: "No, not that. *That I would not do.* " Mark says firmly. "Why would I?

I wouldn't do that for anyone.

So don't worry."

Sebastian: "But that is what she wants, as I am a psychic, I can feel it, she will not be satisfied with *little*. She will not be satisfied with *less*.

She wants something, something that will be for her to keep. She wants you.

She wants *Charlie*.

Her love.

And for some inexplicable reason, or one I cannot fathom yet, she sees you as him.

She wants you to take his place. Be her *all*.

It does sound *nice*...but at the same time it will take everything away from you.

Everything else you have left.

It's quiet.

He continues: "Whoever he was...

She must have loved him.

She must have wanted him.

She is still waiting for him, to join her. Help with her sorrow and wanting.

Or maybe she just wants *you in his* place."

"Or she just wants <u>me</u>," Mark replies.

Sebastian: "...She seems perfect. As if everything you ever wanted, needed. She is probably, thus the emotion of last night.

She will take you out of all of it...to be her company, be her lover!

Someone she can laugh with."

A long lost love. Lost long ago, 70 years ago.

"And laughed at," Mark adds coyly.

"If she is a ghost...then she is not alive anymore. What can she do to harm me?" he takes it as a dare. "I'm in control. I will not let her do harm to me.

I will take only what I want from her.

I am in control."

Mark repeated it as if to persuade Sebastian of the truth of it, but Sebastian still wasn't buying it.

So he continues: "There is nothing more she can want from me. Nothing more than what I'm willing to give to her. I can't give anything I don't want to - not my life, not anything. I'm sure of that.

I can protect myself.

And even though I can't remember her most of the time...

She is thinking that she has me under control! Ha! That is where she is mistaken.

A little excitement, a little love affair...

I want that. That is what I want.

But nothing more. That is it.

Whilst Mark is being so strong, and sure of his feelings, he changes his moods quickly.

Dreamily again:

"I need to see her. I need to see her again. Feel her... But not far away from the hotel.

Not at the sea. She wants me to go to the ocean with her.

I will not."

He is sitting next to him on the white sofa, suddenly with all valor he leans closer to him, to his face, and begs: "Please Sebastian, you must help <u>me</u>.

I know that you are here for <u>me</u>."

His face is touching Sebastian's, his cheek, then lowering it onto his shoulder, Marks thick dark hair brushing him and tickling him on the back of his neck.

Even though Sebastian is surprised at first it does feel normal, natural to him, nice.

Then Mark leans back.

"*I must go back to my room.*

I can't stay here."

He is gone like the wind, not even Sebastian can catch him.

And he locks himself in his room, waiting for the night to come.

Eighteenth Chapter

Saturday 2nd November, early morning
All Souls' Day
Mark

IN THE MORNING, MARK WAKES. She didn't come to visit him this night.

He knows that when he wakes up.

Alone in his own bed.

The curtains are half drawn and the balcony doors are open.

They open now all the way back, and then suddenly the doors are slightly ajar again.

They move in an unforeseeable rhythm - open, close.

But quietly, like a ghost. He's sure the door is not waking up the neighbouring room. The fresh sea breeze is coming in as gusts of wind.

Making him cold.

He goes to close it just in his sleeping attire.

He knows she wasn't here tonight.

But he had left the door open!

For her to come in.

She was not here.

Mark is nervous and wistful, yearning for…

He walks around the room.
There is something that he is not giving her.
She wants something different?
Is he not enough?

Nineteenth Chapter

Saturday 2nd November, breakfast time
Sebastian

THE NEXT MORNING AT BREAKFAST, SEBASTIAN IS WAITING FOR MARK. No show.

He goes to his room. No reply.

He has already *gone*, they tell him at Reception.

Has Mark forgotten the whole night and their talk in the evening together?

He has gone and joined the party, driving out of the hotel, further away, towards the seashore.

Even before breakfast.

Twentieth Chapter

Saturday 2ⁿᵈ November,
still early morning, before breakfast time
Mark

AFTER AN EARLY BREAKFAST IN HIS ROOM MARK FEELS OK, LIKE NOTHING IS HAPPENING, A FRESH NEW DAY. He closes the balcony door again, forgets why it was even open, puts on fresh clothes. It is a big day ahead of him.

Today they are going golfing.
And he must join them. Must look his best.
Must behave the best.

The birthday girl's father will be there as well. He is joining them for the day. He is a big fish in the company. In the city.

This is Mark's chance. *This is why he is here.* To make a good impression.

To try and make something of himself.

He is just so glad that he got invited. Not many people pay that much attention to him normally, even now.

There is something telling him not to go. A soft nagging feeling. He soon puts it to the back of his mind.

They're going golfing up in the north of the country, to a famous golf course, right by the sea. A hidden gem set on an incredibly breathtaking strip of linksland along the Atlantic Coast. It has become well-known to a select few seeking challenging golf. You can try driving your ball straight to the green, but if you are too long it just might end up going over one of the cliffs.

What a beautiful place to be.

This is the place he needs to be.

And fun company.

A soft nagging feeling that he is forgetting something, missing something, this small ache in his heart...

Twenty-first Chapter

Saturday 2nd November, after lunch
Sebastian

SEBASTIAN IS STARTING TO GET NERVOUS. He's walking around the house, the hotel grounds, anxious. The party is gone, at least most of them.

The loose stones are crunching beneath his feet. It is getting on his nerves. He steps onto the green grass instead. It is slightly wet.

How could he let this happen? They are supposed to be back by now. It is after lunch, but *these things*, they could take much longer...in his experience. When he asks some people left behind, the lazy ones who didn't want to join, they just laugh... *They will be there till sundown.*

"There is a reason why we are at the hotel ...", the girl says to her partner. On his arm, she is hanging slightly as they walk by, now talking more amongst themselves. "... so we don't get frozen to the bones all day at games like these." These people are in the know.

"...or soaking wet!" Calls out the boy, aiming his fingers at the clouds.

There are dark clouds gathering. "There's going to be a big storm"

Sebastian looks up. *Just what he needs!*

There are more reasons for his dread. He feels it on his skin. One of them is explained - the dampness in the air. The pressure outside, slowly changing. The acoustics, the sounds, growing stronger around them.

The peace before the storm.

But it is not supposed to come until later tonight. The downpour.

He sees a flock of geese fly by in a mock panic, as if they also got the news.

Trying to make their getaway, before it gets wild.

They must leave tonight - at the latest. Outride the storm.

In the car. He is sure they can make it.

How could he have slept through it like this? *He slept like the dead - as if he couldn't have been woken up. What has he been doing all night? He couldn't remember.*

He felt so tired.

When he got up, it was 10 o'clock already, still in time for breakfast. He shouldn't have let him out of his sight, he wasn't supposed to. What was so *important* to Mark that he had to go with them? He hoped that it was worth it... Abandoning their plans all together...

Leaving him here like this, all alone, no explanation, no word from him. Even though he had agreed on their plan the evening before. That didn't seem to be like him... Then it had dawned upon him - what if Mark really didn't remember?

Not remember their plan, their conversation - at all? So he wasn't coming back home any time soon. With no reason to hurry... Well...that went through Sebastian like a new sense of dread.

That is probably what had happened.

And how could he, Sebastian, forget... the situation? He was dazed.

He overlooked it as a small detail.

What is happening... to him?

He felt cold, he had to go into the building, he used the back-door entrance, the soft carpeting soon underneath his feet. Sebastian remembers Mark was sure about one thing: nobody could control him - not even him, Sebastian. Protect him from his own foolishness, Sebastian was growing angry, yet afraid at the same time.

He heads back to the library.

He goes again through the box he has hidden here, looking for something he might have missed. One file of papers had stuck together.

Suddenly a copy of an old police report, he hasn't seen before. Old...from the 30's. Her photograph, again staring back at him.

The room... it used to be Charlie's.

Charlie... and *what was he like?*

Now he finds an exact date, finally. The date, 2nd November, All Saints' Day. Seventy years ago to this day, information he hadn't seen before.

It had happened.

The tragedy had not happened on All Hallows' Eve... it was today. As Mark has said, he was in fact correct. As... was the ghost.

But Sebastian *didn't* know…the gossip columns all said it happened on Halloween, embellished it to their liking.… Made it into a story. But this - this in fact.

The old paper was now crumbling and swaying in his hands.

But it held the facts. Finally.

The location and description of the room, unique in its way in the house. The date. The photograph. It had happened during the night of All Souls Day.

He heard Church bells ringing far way.

Which is tonight.

Here it is. The date. It happened tonight.

As Mark had said:

"….in two days, he will kill me…"

A sense of dread and uneasiness came through him, once more.

The others, they didn't even make to All Souls' Eve… alive.

He must get him in the car and get him away - at any cost! Even asleep, even at night!

The whole day is suddenly gone by and a dark light is slowly setting in.

How did that happen?

He loves her oh so completely. And the wind and the rain are setting in the countryside, slowly but surely. His wet feet and pants…*he said it was raining heavily yesterday,* how is it possible?

It wasn't, at all. It is going to be today?

How could Mark have been caught up in the storm *already*?

It's like she has been bending time around - what happened yesterday was today, what was in the past, was in the present now.

Her suddenly in full flesh, looking beautiful at the party. Like in the old days.

Sebastian was getting confused. He was losing sense of all the things around him, of time.

Twenty-second Chapter

Ratmulen House, 1927

As she moved - her crystal earrings were dazzling. *Moved to look at <u>him</u>.*

Lifting her head, looking deep into his hazel eyes.

They were supposed to meet that night. In the room with the balcony stairs conveniently leading down into the garden outside, to freedom. His room.

Twenty-third Chapter

SUDDENLY, HE DOESN'T KNOW WHERE HE IS. He's going straight to the sea. *The fresh air finally, he welcomes it, with a sense of eagerness.* It is dark, rain on his neck, he knows where to go. He knows where to turn next. *In a straight line, he is heading for the ocean, through the sand dunes to the beating of the waves.* The sound is roaring in his ears.

Water and bits of salt in his mouth.

Through the wood, he had gone...taking small paths, secret shortcuts...that postpone his journey, he is lost.

But he has his direction and he knows where to go.

He's going to her.

Him, Sebastian.

Not Mark.

Not Charlie.

All of that. It suddenly became clear to Sebastian:

Mark really doesn't want to sacrifice himself for anyone, he is just too selfish for that.

He couldn't care that much for anyone really, at least not yet, so it seems.

To the sea, that is the only place Estrella wants to go, and take her precious, weak victims...to achieve her goals... Which are what exactly?

That Mark will never do - his own spot on intuition tells him otherwise. And he has been able to protect himself until now.

And she knows that.

Oh, how he, Mark, is in love with her. He is fascinated by her, yes! But never subordinate to her, never that. That was a mistake in her thinking, and in Sebastian's.

It is all about someone that is more open to her. That is what she is looking for.

But Sebastian - yes - he is more open to help "people" like her.

She feels that. She already knows.

He lets her inside of him, gives her access - to all he is.

Twenty-fourth Chapter

Ratmulen House 1927 / 1996
Estrella

SHE'S WAITING FOR TONIGHT, LOOKING AT THE HOUSE.
He, Sebastian, gave her that power. Even if unknowingly.
Now, she can do so much more.

Charlie was such a sweet boy, the heart of all her desire,
someone who would be sweet to her, or rather she could
take care of him. Such a good-hearted soul, so boyish,
innocent in his nature. He is all she needs.

She must have him back. *She will have him back tonight.*
To cherish him. To cherish her.

He loved her also...so completely.

The others... they were weak! *Tonight, she will go for*
him.

She will wait for him.
Charlie... He will come to her.
Sebastian, he *feels that. He lets her inside of him.*
Makes contact with her - like at the party.

Let's her accomplish, do things... she wouldn't even
dream of before, without him. His energy, his life-force!
The dancing, his looks, the fun...

The others are seeing her now - and even talking to her.

It is all because of him.

His power.

She takes it, uses it for herself...and he doesn't even know it.

She took her aim at him - she knows.

Almost ever since the first moment she met Sebastian.

She found how to take advantage of his unique abilities and use it for herself.

And he lets her, unknowingly, unwillingly. The thing is...she doesn't need his approval! He is giving Estrella the space she needs, the power. All the same he is losing it - to her.

Being a puppet to her will, as a consequence.

He is opening all the doors for her.

But is he the one who she is after or not, in the end...?

She will use him, Sebastian, he will unwittingly sacrifice himself for her. He is strong enough - and durable to make it all the way **to the sea**.

Sebastian is something different. He is powerful.

Estrella can feel that **he will** do that for her.

Now that he is under her spell, her influence.

She will make him want to sacrifice for her – happily - and he won't even know what he is doing. Their connection, their shared open channel, is now that strong.

He is not like all the others, she met, over the years... here at the hotel. He will endure the trip to the sea...not like the rest. She laughs: She's luring him like a moth to the flame.

The strong one. The one that will endure.

But he is not the one **who she** wants.

Sebastian...will come.

HE....will follow after him.

Estrella knows that, she feels that in her all too frail, pale body and trembling heart.

She needs him here tonight.

At the shore.

With her, *oh, she loves him* so much.

The guest, the hotel visitor in the room that was once hers.

How beautiful he is...

Charlie.

He has the recklessness, foolishness, irresponsibility in him, the wild heart that she needs.

Like her Charlie.

In this room, there he was waiting for her, that fateful night to leave together and never look back. They will... tonight.

She: Charlene, she wasn't a man. Was that a misrepresentation or miscalculation on her part? Estrella didn't want her.

She promised me love eternal. Her touch so soft on my skin. So unexpected, nothing I had ever known before... So I went outside.

"She was not a man! They called her Charlie, but she was not ... <u>him</u>."

I couldn't get into her room, I had to lure her outside, she didn't let me in. She was not Charlie. He, he is waiting for me, waiting on me, still.

And the other man, further back in time, feels like ages ago. Felt like he was for her. The so good-looking man, who strayed into the woods. He was out to rob the hotel and its guests - he got into the hotel through the room with the balcony, the same one, took advantage of it.

That man tried to resist her!

He was laughing at her: "You are not real! – you are not a woman for me..." He mocked her.

And oh...what an ending he got. He deserved all of it! For treating her that way.

He got what was coming to him. She lured him deeper and deeper.

He is just like him... brown mushy hair and a big-wide reindeer eyes.

Sweet and appealing.

Not like the other.

Sebastian's powers gave her more energy, and at the same time he has more ability to last and be the one to follow through. He is resilient and resistant.

She will use him only as bait.

Use him and throw him away. She doesn't want him.

Just *Charlie*.

Mark?

He will come to save him, and while doing so, sacrifice himself for him.

It is just a trap.

Twenty-fifth Chapter

THE VELVETY SUN IS LAYING ITS LAST RAYS ONTO THE OPEN VAST FAIRWAYS OF THE GOLF COURSE.

The most beautiful color of gold and real Irish emerald green one has ever seen.

He is blown away by the sheer beauty on the course, the sky and the water. At the last hole a gust of wind blows his ball after a promising swing into a heavy rough on the edge. While he is trying to get it out, get himself back into a good mood, suddenly the ball bounces over... Mark just stands there in awe gazing on, as it disappears into the dark oceans below.

The game has gone on for too long...it is getting dark soon.

The days are not so long here now in November.

The sea is calm, gray and the color of charcoal, ready for a storm.

The party gets back to the hotel. It must be before dinner.

Mark is nervous, uneasy.

How can it be so late?

Dark all around him.

Suddenly it is before midnight. The full moon outside is now hidden in the clouds.

Mark is walking around his room, half in a dream, he knows he must *do something.*

He was supposed *to be doing something.*

How could he have forgotten?

How the day has gone by so quickly. *Was he sleeping just now...*

Outside it is pitch black. It is so quiet - nobody is looking for him. *Nobody is calling out for him.*

As if the whole hotel was dead.

He knows he must do something.

Right now.

Where is Sebastian? *His friend.*

It is all coming back to him, one by one, just a fragment after fragment...

They were supposed to leave together, today.

Not tonight, earlier! But it is already so late and Sebastian is not here.

Is it already after the rain, the storm? He remembers ferocious sprays of water beating against his windows.

Was that when he fell asleep?

He looks outside, there seems to be just a soft drizzle now. But the ground, the balcony, is soaked. A mighty chill goes through him, even though it is so warm inside.

He puts on his coat, his best coat. And his sports shoes.

He must go outside.

He must go looking for him. Outside.

His friend is lost and he must go find him.

Bring him back.

He knows he must help. He just knows it in his soul.

Something is happening. *But not to him.*

He knows where.

He is afraid, but courageous. He must go.

He takes the balcony stairs into the garden.

Unseen.

He is all alone. It is raining slightly.

This is his responsibility.

His doing. Sebastian came here for him to help.

Now nothing is happening to him, but Sebastian is in trouble.

All he wanted is to save him.

This is his, Mark's, responsibility now.

Unselfishly, he must save **him**.

The moon now unhidden is shining on his way. The grass on his walking shoes is cold and sticky. His heart is pounding in his chest, like a runaway train.

He looks up at the full moon, feeling as if it wants to burst right out, with its white light and energy, and spill into the night.

He is taking long breaths in. Long steps, he knows the direction.

Being on automatic. He remembers.

He will always remember that way.

He knows it by heart.

To the ocean. There they will be.

There <u>he</u> will be.

And *he, Mark,* must be there for him.

He let him down *ooh* so completely, so he mustn't do that again now.

He goes straight, a clear line, straight to the sea. Even though here there is no path, he's taking the short way, just to be faster. By using the path his journey would be convenient, but much longer. He knows the way, even though he had never been here, *never been here*.

Never walked this path.

Never seen this part of the sea.

Following his instinct, he knows where to go, where the sea is.

The night, all darkness around him.

Instinctively, he knows that he is on the right path, due west to the ocean. The moon is shining on all the things surrounding him, so he can see around him. The noise, a humming comes from the distance. Then closer.

Through the meadows, the path, bushes, thistles and stubble, open fields - *a part of the beginning in the woods -* he arrives to the first swell of dunes.

Glistening in the night air, still warm, bright.

Through the dunes he makes his way to the beach and the open ocean.

To the water.

The sea mist, dampening the air around.

As if finally, he could breathe.

He is catching his breath. Afraid.

He hears the nearby rumbling of it.

Alone at night with her - he would never, ever go here. For that, he values his life far more. But now - it is different.

Now he has to give something from himself. Being all his fault.

He resisted, he knew - what it meant, somewhere he did inside. *In a way he did.*

On land she couldn't touch someone, not really. She could be *vindictive*, yes...fool a person, but never strong enough. But here she can harness the force of the sea. It's ferociousness, to use.

That strikes without destroying.

He stayed around, he teased her...knew what she wanted.

Knew what he didn't want to give: "*Next time, my love!*" He smiled sweetly at her, catching the amulet on her neck and twisting it around his fingers playfully. "Next time."

Just as they were getting closer... The freshness of the spray almost in the air.

He could feel her disappointment.

What about his shoes?

Vanity, she understood.

Swaying her curls wildly in the wind, she accompanied him back.

Visions, dreamscapes - coming back to him. *Was that really him?* It definitely felt like it.

But now she is succeeding. He is getting closer. Coming within her grasp.

He never did really want to subside to her in real life.

He never did.

*But he definitely knows **she** is like **no-one** he will ever meet - now, or ever, in the future.*

Now his decision is made - it is his affair, he must resolve it, by being there. Being there for him, Sebastian - when he was there for him the other way around.

His shoes full of mud, his legs hurting, he falls into the uneven surprises in the terrain.

The wind is howling, there is no peace at all. The storm is coming again?

Or is it still before the big storm? He is confused, disoriented.

He walks through the untamed tall grasses of the dunes, wet, they keep obstructing him. When he reaches the end of the dunes, he lowers himself down and lands with the beach sand beneath his steps. The sand is crumbling beneath him slightly, making it difficult to walk. But at the same time, it feels reassuring.

<u>*This must be the place.*</u>

Twenty-sixth Chapter

After Midnight
Mark

HER GREEN EYES DAZZLING.

He could almost feel...he could almost feel them on him.

Sebastian - he came here to take care of him, to help. He was called for that. And now, he's going to lose his life over it? That mustn't happen, he won't let it.

What a calming, *caring*, presence, he has been the last few days to him.

For him.

As if he had known him a much longer time. A strange, strange feeling. How is that possible?

And one he is not deserving of.

Being the person that he is. Shallow, vain and careless, so selfish, not really caring about the people around, women, no-one.

As if it was all just a game for him.

But isn't it for everybody? He's just trying to get what is his, *find his place in the world*. Mark was sure he hasn't shown himself in the best light these few days.

That is not who he is, really - he was sure.

But maybe he hasn't found out yet.

It has found *him* now.

In the form of an otherworldly ghost.

From another world, so foreign to this.

To be *this* spellbound. What more could he wish for?

What more could there be in life. Than this, this feeling of being alive.

Being a part of something that matters, that is important and exciting, adventurous.

Maybe all of his life was just fleeting, not important, not yet.

Leading up to this.

This sea and unreal, crisp sand holding his body upward, saving him from drowning, not yet anyway.

To have her, feel her in his arms.

Mark is there walking toward the shore; he sees the glittering ocean. It is vast and black.

<u>He who he is looking for</u> is there on the ground, on the sand.

The waves just touching him, taking him with them.

She's in the water, her dress, the ends of her skirt soaked.

She's leaning towards him.

Mark makes a move toward her, near them. He sees Sebastian is out of himself, knocked out, unconscious, not knowing anything of the world, just lying there.

He feels Sebastian is in danger.

Danger has engulfed him, *his friend*, not himself.

Should she want *him*? Did she choose better? Would that be possible?

He being so much a different, a better man than he was, he was magical.

Almost a magical being, like her.

She must feel drawn to that.

Or is she?

Mark was jealous.

He cares enough to help him: he is going to.

He was here, with him, doing so much for him. To help him.

He is ready, he can sacrifice for him. *Whatever that means.*

But not for her.

They are still friends.

Even though he has forgotten so much. These past few days have gone by so quickly for him.

What wouldn't he give to remember, remember everything about him, and her…everything he forgot. But tonight, all that is coming back to him. Into his mind to keep, not forget. Finally.

He doesn't even know who Sebastian is, where he came from. But he knows that they are friends, he feels it, he remembers it. He likes him, cares for him.

Cares that he is okay…he doesn't even know when this happened, but it did.

Such a strange and unexpected man. Drawn to his life.

So, he does not feel that alone, alone for everything, like he always does.

He, such a pretty boy, with the wickedness inside him… Just lost in the crowd.

Was he there for him all along? Who sent him his direction anyhow?

He will go to him, to the ocean. Find him and with his sacrifice he will open himself up to Estrella.

Give her whatever she wants.

Meet her at the ocean.

He will make it this time. He will arrive, on time.

There is still time to save him, to do something about it.

To change things, to give himself up.

That is what she wants, w*ith all of his soul, his body.*

There she is right in front of him.

In all her mesmerizing beauty.

"Take me.

It is me you want anyhow."

She replies to that with a kittenish smile:

"No problem..." she is very smooth.

He is watching her, as if seeing her for the first time, yet with all this familiarity he feels about her. *She is his lover, after all.*

He takes a step closer to her. His legs, trousers, in the water.

Even closer. Towards her now.

The spray of the ocean again on his lips. *How can one forget.*

He feels everything, even the again-starting rain on his cheeks.

His head is full of poetry.

He smells the scent of the ocean, the water and seaweeds, he is sorting through them, and her perfume sweet like a melody. Sugary, ringing out, heady...heavy.

He steps a bit closer, that moment, oh is he charmed by her.

She is like a fairy, a princess, *a fairy-tale come true.*

"We will be together finally." she whispers against the beating waves.

A ringing melody going on and on in his ears ... and his heart?

She: her whole body in the water, he is stunned, he feels the icy cold on his body.

The waves are freezing him cold and engulfing him.

When they are standing there together, the ocean is suddenly calm. He stops, pauses, startled. He is taken aback.

But he is standing between her, the ocean, and Sebastian on the sand. He is safe. From her?

"Come closer!" she calls out.

Like a siren to unknowing sailors. Yet he is not that innocent.

He steps so close now.

She embraces, engulfs him, carries him into a sweet, velvety, passionate kiss.

He doesn't want to, now he doesn't, but he is drawn in by her. As if absorbed by her.

Finally, she has him where she wants. The lonely ghost.

He starts touching her, embracing passionately, back at her.

He doesn't know who he is, he doesn't know where he is, he doesn't know what...

The not that faraway trees, watching the scene, sing eternally with beauty.

The wind from the distant mountains is coming.

He only knows that for him, there is no another way. Forward, on...

They are struggling with each other slightly.

They are moving together into the part of the water where it is still very shallow, just embracing their feet.

Dressed in evening wear. *A dazzling frock, for a dazzling end.*

Her hair is falling loose from her ribbons, in a flight of passion.

She is caressing him; he is holding her. Touching. Feeling the magic...

Kissing him, touching him, she brings him onto his back, he is lying down on the wet sand of the shoreline.

He is still in the water though, just an inch from touching his face, still such bliss he is feeling. She, lowers herself onto his body. Sits on top of him. In this delicate dance, her legs spread under her skirt around him. They are making love.

Here in the ocean, in the water, she has finally come to her full force.

On the contrary for Mark, who is dizzy and weak...and so enthralled with her.

At the same time Estrella start to strangle him with her delicate hands, placing them around his neck.

In the heights of their passion, he is so...so enchanted by her.

She is making him soaked more and more, moving towards the deeper water. The water is rising, flooding everything all around them.

The white foam of waves just going through them tenderly...

Underneath the water.

She is pressing her body to his more and more, pressing him towards the ground beneath them.

Her hands now firmly against his throat.

She finally wins, she is getting what she wants.

Him for herself, and only for herself.

She is killing Mark, drowning him.

He did after all come to her, of his own will.

Oh, such a beautiful night, she is thinking.

Twenty-seventh Chapter

Sunday 3rd November, early morning
Sebastian

IT IS VERY EARLY IN THE MORNING.

The cries of the seagulls are clamorous.

The sun is just coming up, from behind the clouds, breaking out above the sea.

Opening up a new day.

The sweet aroma of the morning, after a long rainy night. And the smell of seawater.

Sebastian wakes. He is ok. Soaked to the very last bit.

Otherwise, he is alright. Checking himself.

He is lying on the sand.

His head hurts. Tremendously.

A few meters from him there is lying Mark, he is dead.

The police are arriving.

Sebastian is startled, they are not giving him space to breathe.

Somebody alerted them already.

They are taking Mark's body, strangled. Bruises around his neck.

They are taking Sebastian to jail. *The police station.* Arresting him…

Charging him for murder.

The only thing left: to yell. Helplessly, lifelessly.

Without no control over anything:

"No, I didn't do this.

That was her.

She did it!

She took him away from us."

As the police are dragging him away, through the beach, with force.

"I tried to prevent this."

He cries almost.

"I didn't manage to prevent this. Stop this.

My friend!"

There is nothing, the beach is empty.

Just this nagging saltiness down his throat.

Tears mirroring and heating in his eyes. The wind calmed down.

The cloud covered everything.

The detectives, taking him with them.

For the next few days, there is talk about it everywhere…

It is a huge scandal throughout the hotel, the main town and all of its surroundings.

For Sebastian it is sounds buzzing around him, from anywhere and everywhere, from outer worlds, he cannot place it.

He is in the jail at the police station for several days.

Then he is released from custody and the charges are dropped, because it is proven that the bruises on Mark's neck were indeed done by somebody else's hand, not his.

He really didn't do it, they believe him.

They let him walk.

It was done by a woman's hand.

They are looking *for her – the woman.*

They are looking for the mystery woman. Everybody has seen her – yes.

Can anybody describe her – no. Her image is blurring, nothing is ever the same when they speak... They have never really seen her, not up close. Who was she?

Was she a guest at the hotel? The *members of his party speak.*

They don't know. Nobody can identify what she looked like indeed.

With the woman from the big party, nobody is connecting that to her.

...as if they have forgotten about her completely.

Sebastian says nothing, to anything really.

He doesn't talk about the ghost.

He isn't able to recall anything from that night.

Or remember.

How did he, Sebastian, get to the beach?

He doesn't remember.

Mark.

What transpired.

Maybe he will.

Epilogue

Six months later
May 1996, late afternoon
Ratmulen House
Sebastian

HE IS SITTING AT THE WRITING DESK AT THE RATMULEN HOTEL.
It is coming to the end of May, the beginning of summer.

Sebastian has just arrived for a few days, to get some work done in peace on his new project.

Outside it is lovely, much different weather than usual. The birds are singing and there is a pleasant, still warm breeze coming in through the open door to the iron balcony.

It is coming up to dusk, yet he does not see the sun set from the direction of the windows.

Just a long golden shadow setting in on the desk.

But he can still see his writing.

It does feel strange being here, at the same direct spot of his, Mark's, room again, just like no time has passed at all. Yet he had to come.

He is tired. He puts down his pen, his hand aching.

Suddenly the light curtain on the window moves slightly, letting in a scent of fresh linen.

And a breath of fresh air.

The luxurious material is almost non-existent, yet it is now moving in the wind, uplifting itself completely.

Nearly touching Sebastian at his desk, putting a shade on his writing. He lifts his head.

He knew what this meant.

He left the doors slightly open.

He is waiting for him calmly.

Mark is sitting on the desk edge now, nearly no weight at all. Dressed completely in the best evening wear one can imagine for himself.

He looks the part, beautiful, almost hauntingly.

The black suit, dark as a midnight obsidian, bow tie with sharp edges, all laying on a snow-white shirt, ending with the perfect silver cufflinks.

He is smiling at him.

He stepped inside, from the balcony.

A slight breeze from the outside.

Through the open doors.

Unheard, unseen by the world.

Not a sound to be heard, until he says:

"Thank you for coming. To see me."

Sebastian smiles affectionately, his face turned towards the desk, then lifts his head to see him finally fully for the first time.

He is more beautiful than ever before.

His sharp features, so calm!

Now he answers:

"Of course. I miss you.
How are you doing, really?"
"Good. Great.
It is great to see you."
He speaks low with a pleasurable intensity.
Sebastian comes here every once in a while.
This is the only place where he can see him.
The place where it all started. Being together.
Sebastian remarks, hopefully:
"I hope this time you have more time to spend with
me..."
Sebastian is looking for the connection between them
to grow stronger.
Needing that. He will make that happen.
His friend skips the answer.
Instead, he says:
"She did succeed. I love her.
I would do anything for her. And I am.
And she loves me.
I am like she wanted me to be, who she wanted me to
be...how she wanted.
She takes care of me.
I am hers.
I am happy.
And she is mine."
Soft lilac wisterias outside the windows smell sweet and
intoxicating.

How beautiful this is.

This place.

He laughs happily, like a child, the soft melody ringing in the room.

Vibrating the soft cream-pink walls.

Sebastian feels this warms his heart too.

The man in front of him. The way he feels...so ghostly really.

Yet it is all to Sebastian.

Being so close by him. Close to him.

He is at some sort of peace with him.

Feels no regrets.

This is how it should be...

And he has a friend...forever in a way.

"...what are you working on?"

The ambience around them is relaxed, feels how it should. The time goes slower, as if the old antique clock on the decorated mantle...sounds like it stopped ticking.

Being so close to him, even in this form. To start a relationship, who knew that he finally may get his wish. With a ghost.

Sebastian looks down, at his papers, looking over his work, rustling about. He answers:

"Oh...a story actually.

It is to be about you.

I am nearly finished, Mark..."

On the table his visitor is kicking out his feet into the air, his shoes so well-shined they are like two black lakes, catching the sunlight. He interrupts:

"Oh, it is Charlie now.
You can call me Charlie.
She likes it better like that. "
He says with a shy smile.

All Hallows' Tide

THE EXACT ORIGIN OF *ALL HALLOWS' EVE* IS UNCERTAIN. Some scholars say its origin is Christian whereas others maintain it originated from the Celtic pagan festival '*Samhain*'.

Arising independently as a part of a Christian holiday and vigil for the 'hallows' meaning sacred or holy people, or perhaps developed from *Samhain* to ease Celtic conversion to Christianity. Overall, both geneses are steeped in tradition focusing on love, death and religion.

Christian celebrations over centuries took the form of a much celebrated three-day vigil known as <u>All Hallows' Tide</u> dedicated to honoring saints and hallows – a collective name for *All Hallows' Eve* followed by *All Hallows' Day* (or *All Saints' Day*), and then *All Souls' Day*. The word "hallow" meaning saint, or sanctified.

Many traditions were associated with the notion of purgatory as it was believed that on All Hallows' Eve souls wandered the earth until All Souls' Day before crossing into Heaven.

Traditions like ringing church bells helped the souls find their way, calmed and cleansed; parishioners praying out loud through the forests, and candles aflame served as a light for those languishing souls in the darkness looking for their way back home. Traditions were centred around the graves and graveyards, the French believing that once a year the dead rose for a wild carnival.

Successively during this time on *All Hallows' Tide* people began visiting door-to-door, offering to pray for the departed souls and receiving so called "soul cakes" as sustenance in exchange, being often disguised in masks hoping to hide or mislead possible souls out seeking retribution that night. This baking and sharing of soul cakes was said to conceive trick-or-treating...

Samhain, taking place on October 31 and November 1, celebrated in Ireland since the Middle Ages and continued to this day, welcomes the harvest and ushers in the dark half of the year, and so it is thought that during this time the barriers between the physical and spirit world dissolve. The boundaries between the living and the dead are thinned, which makes it easier for the souls of the departed to visit the living. Also probably being able to visit their former home, where they are welcome. Celts believed beings called 'Aos Sí', meaning the supernatural race, visited earth; offerings were presented to keep the land and harvest protected. Particularly in Ireland and Britain, games took place after the offerings. Commonly these games foretold the future or gained further insight.

Equally, fire acted as ritual and divination. Flame, smoke and ash were said to protect and cleanse. Torches were carried around homes and farms, mimicking the sun and its power of growth, defending against the dark decay of

Winter. In Wales and Ireland, bonfires were lit to prevent the souls of the dead from falling to earth.

Jack-o-lanterns were lit representing the dead, guiding them home as well as a deflection of evil souls. The Gaels would carve a turnip, which later on continued with the use of a pumpkin.

The word Halloween is a shortened version of the wording of the name *Hallows' Eve*. *All Hallows' Eve* was shortened to *Hallowe'en*, and later to *Halloween*.

Notes

Notes

Notes

Notes

Illustrations by
Rachel Mills – page 29, 60, 111, 128, 184
Abigail Burden – page i, 92, 122, 140

Book Layout & eBook Conversion
by manuscript2ebook.com
Cover by Joetherasakdhi

Visit the website:
www.barbara-cooper.net

Lightning Source UK Ltd.
Milton Keynes UK
UKHW020732090223
416597UK00012B/610